CARMEL BIRD

THE BLUEBIRD CAFÉ

ABOUT *UNTAPPED*

Most Australian books ever written have fallen out of print and become unavailable for purchase or loan from libraries. This includes important local and national histories, biographies and memoirs, beloved children's titles, and even winners of glittering literary prizes such as the Miles Franklin Literary Award.

Supported by funding from state and territory libraries, philanthropists and the Australian Research Council, *Untapped* is identifying Australia's culturally important lost books, digitising them, and promoting them to new generations of readers. As well as providing access to lost books and a new source of revenue for their writers, the *Untapped* collaboration is supporting new research into the economic value of authors' reversion rights and book promotion by libraries, and the relationship between library lending and digital book sales. The results will feed into public policy discussions about how we can better support Australian authors, readers and culture.

See untapped.org.au for more information, including a full list of project partners and rediscovered books.

Readers are reminded that these books are products of their time. Some may contain language or reflect views that might now be found offensive or inappropriate.

Like an echo in a valley or a ripple on the surface of a pond, the animal was dying out.

Phoenix Mean

In the beginning was Meaning.

Goethe, *Faust*

ACKNOWLEDGEMENTS

The author and publisher gratefully acknowledge the following sources:

The Lost Childhood and other essays by Graham Greene (Penguin Books, 1962); *The Red Lamp of Incest* by Robin Fox (Hutchinson & Co., 1980); *How It Is* by Samuel Beckett (Grove Press, 1964); *The Hermit in Van Dieman's Land* by Henry Savery (University of Queensland Press, 1964); *Pale Fire* by Vladimir Nabokov (Weidenfield & Nicholson, 1962); *Collected Poems of W. B. Yeats* (Macmillan and Co., 1950) for 'The Stolen Child'.

The author gratefully acknowledges the generous support of the Literature Board of the Australia Council.

CONTENTS

BOOK ONE ·
SAVAGE PARADISE

I was the shadow of the waxwing slain By the false azure in the windowpane.

Vladimir Nabokov, *Pale Fire*

Cataract Hill

The best way to get a good view of the Historic Museum Village of Copperfield is to hire a Fly-By-Nite helicopter. From the night sky you see that Copperfield is covered by a gigantic glass dome through which shine the millions of lights that line the edges and decorate the surfaces of the buildings. People who have seen an oil refinery at night nearly always say Copperfield looks like an oil refinery trapped under glass. Or is that plastic, they say. It must be plastic. They see a monstrous dome, like a snow dome in which the models of people have come to life and where trees and flowers really grow. The surface of the dome is cleaned inside and out every morning by a system of detergent jets and hot-water hoses and fans. The ventilation system of the dome has been described as the ultimate miracle of modern engineering.

Copperfield is on top of Cataract Hill which overlooks the Gorge where the South Esk meets the North Esk to form the Tamar River at the city of Launceston in northern Tasmania. The Gorge is a huge rift between cliffs of black volcanic rock. The sides of the rift are almost vertical, and between them, four hundred feet below, the water froths across a barrier of rock, forming a cataract. In former times Cataract Hill was occupied by a suburb called Trevallyn where steep streets wound through a forest of English and Tasmanian trees and where prosperous families lived in large houses made from timber and stone. The timber houses were tall and rambling and decorated with verandahs and fretwork: the stone houses were built from blocks of golden sandstone and resembled Georgian dolls' houses. The suburb of Trevallyn had to be removed to make way for Copperfield.

Copperfield has attracted more visitors to the island than could have been thought possible. The Premier said he never in his wildest dreams imagined it would be like this. The Governor said it was like a dream come true. The Mayor of Launceston said it was the answer to his prayers. *Time* called it the Disneyland of the Antarctic; *Life* said it was the only genuine time-warp in the southern hemisphere. People who have never heard of Tasmania have heard of the Historic Museum Village of Copperfield. A large fleet of luxury ferries now brings visitors from the mainland of Australia; the airport at Launceston has been enlarged and made to resemble the Paris airport. Lovers come from Japan, California, Sweden and everywhere else to be married in one of the churches in Copperfield, or in the little Temple of the Eye of God.

The Historic Museum Village is the most successful business of a company called The Best People that is owned by Nancy, Bill and Oliver Best. The Bests grew up in Launceston, on the low river flats where the streets were narrow and treeless, where the houses were timber cottages lacking verandahs, lacking fretwork. The paint used to peel and the roofs used to leak.

In 1929 when the Bests were children, the river rose and submerged the houses on the flats, and the Best family had to be rescued from the roof of their house. Their dog was drowned. The marks left by the receding flood waters could never be removed from the wallpaper, and remained, rusty and wavy, until the house was demolished in 1975 to make way for a motel.

After the flood Mrs Best put up a framed photograph above the mantelpiece in the kitchen. The photograph was from the newspaper and it showed all the Bests on the roof of their house which was surrounded by water. The top of a distant tree poked up through the surface, and a dead animal could be seen floating on the forlorn lake that covered the earth. The photograph had appeared in the newspaper with the caption 'Irene and George Beast and family on the roof of their Invermay home'.

'For God's sake, Irene,' George Best said, 'cut the bloody words off before you start hanging up the flaming picture where the whole bloody world can see it. George Beast, George Beast. It makes me sick. The paper makes me sick. You cut that off or you'll be sorry.' Irene left the words; George did nothing. Nancy, Bill and Oliver—who became The Best People—never pretended they did not come from Invermay.

In her office, Nancy has the photograph of the Best family on the roof of their house. Whenever she is interviewed on television she has her two dalmatians, Rags and Riches, with her, and she always talks about her humble childhood, and always speaks of the flood.

'The people next door caught typhoid,' she says, 'and two of the children died. My brothers and I began our first business at that time. You see, the local chemist, Mr Quinlan, stayed in the rooms above his shop during the flood, and the water came lapping over the top of the stairs and onto the landing. It must have been terrible up there, but he refused to be rescued. Now imagine all the little bottles of brightly coloured remedies being swept from the shelves and washed out with the water. All these bottles were stranded in the gutters when the waters receded. Well, my brothers and I salvaged all these things and we got a wheelbarrow from somewhere,' Nancy waves her hand as she says this, and bends over to stroke the ears of Riches, 'from somewhere, and then we went round selling them to people.'

'What was in the bottles?'

'Oh, you know, cures for snake bite, bronchitis, corns, warts, earache, chilblains, boils. Everything. Anything. Some of the bottles didn't have labels because they had washed off.'

'So what did you do with those?'

'I made some labels—For External Use Only—and sold them as a cure for nasal catarrh. Apparently they worked quite well if you mixed them with boiling water and inhaled the steam with your head under a towel. I've often wished I knew what was in those bottles.'

When Nancy was fifteen she started working at the Launceston woollen mill, but she soon moved on to live with a man who owned a caravan park.

'I became interested in caravan parks, and I began to see the wonderful possibilities of tourism. I managed a caravan park at Devonport for a time, and then I bought a caravan park, and later a motel and a travel agency. Then Bill and I (Bill had finished law by this time), we started the theatrical side of the business. We've brought everything to Tasmania—everything from the Old Vic to the most incredible freak shows. But of course the most exciting project has been the Historic Museum Village.'

'Did you think of that?'

'I suppose I did, really. But the key person in the whole operation was my brother, Oliver. You see, he is the architect who designed the dome. Without the dome Copperfield would be just another theme park.' She smiled and looked down at the dogs. 'Well, not quite as bad as that. But I know that without the dome the place could not be what it is.'

As well as having Copperfield, The Best People have a television station, a brewery, a cemetery, a health farm, an art gallery, an airline, a shipping line, a computer company, three newspapers, and a magazine called Best.

The Historic Museum Village of Copperfield was inspired by the original town of Copperfield on the Welcome River in the far north-west of Tasmania at Cape Grim. The original town is now a ghost town where wild bees build their hives in the

tabernacle on the altar of St Brendan's Church. The Copperfield beneath the dome on Cataract Hill reproduces and brings
to life the old Copperfield of the forties and fifties.

From the helicopter you can see the twinkling outlines of the
copper mine, the miners' cottages, the large houses of the rich
people, the grand houses of the managers. The main street has
the school, the churches, the theatre, the court house, the general store, the Palace Hotel, the Welcome Stranger Hotel, the
Abel Magwitch Hotel. It has the town hall, the railway station
and the Bluebird Café.

Larger than these replicas of old buildings and more wonderful are the casino, the ferris wheel, the big dipper, the
scenic railway, the merry-go-round, the convict ship and the
waxworks. Besides these traditional features of the amusement
park, the Historic Museum Village also contains reconstructed
limestone caves, and reproductions of Cradle Mountain and
the Savage River where visitors can go canoeing or climbing. A
horse tram goes from the copper mine out to Suicide Bay.

The lights on all the buildings are white, strung out like
strands of pearls. On the roof of the Bluebird Café, and visible
only from the air, is the outline of a soaring swallow described
in lights which are the blue of burning gas.

The Bluebird Café

You can buy scale models of the Bluebird Café, or a kit from
which you can assemble your own model. These are made
from fibreglass, wood, polystyrene, cardboard or paper. The fibreglass models can be fitted with a working musical box that
plays the popular old melody 'Bluebird of Happiness'. Unpaint-
ed models should be enamelled with Floquil Conrail Blue and
trimmed with Diesel Dark Blue. A sheet of custom-made dry
transfers for the signs 'Lunches, Dinners, Teas, Bluebird Café,
Bushells' can be purchased separately.

Copperfield

The country around the original town of Copperfield is treacherous and forbidding. It was described by early explorers as
'practically impenetrable and wholly uninhabitable'. Copper
was discovered there in 1872 by Philosopher Smith. After this,
people came to live in the wild, dark hills. They felled the trees,
cleared the slopes, built houses, gardens and shops.

By 1985 Copperfield had become a ghost town where only
one person lived. This was a woman called Bedrock Mean.

The Means

The first Mean to come to Tasmania was Abijah who arrived in
Queenstown, a mining settlement on the west coast, in 1869. He
started the Palace Hotel which was later run by his son, Tobias,
and then by his grandson, Philosopher (who had been named
after Philosopher Smith). The Palace burnt down in 1913. Philosopher Mean's son was born on the night of the fire, and was
consequently named Phoenix. When Phoenix was one month
old, Philosopher left Queenstown and sailed north with his wife
and baby son. They rounded Cape Grim and made their way up
the Welcome River until they came to Copperfield where they
established another Palace Hotel, and later the Bedrock Press
and the Bluebird Café. Phoenix Mean grew up in Copperfield,
and he married the daughter of the man who ran the theatre.
Their children were twins and they named the boy Carrillo
after a singer who came to the town in 1939, and they named
the girl Bedrock after the Mean family press. Bedrock had a
daughter who was named, in the fashion of the flower children
of the sixties, Lovelygod. Lovelygod, the last of the Means, disappeared at the age of ten. She became one of those mysterious
and tragic Australian children who vanish, leaving no trace.

The Letter

When the Palace Hotel in Queenstown burnt down in 1913, the family were not able to save many things. One thing that did survive was the fragment of a letter written in 1869 by Abijah just before he left England.

'I was walking along Park Lane,' it said, 'on the eastern side of Hyde Park, with the child Tobias on my shoulders, when I became aware of a man who was dogging my footsteps. I kept up a steady pace for some distance, and as I was passing the Dog & Partridge, I saw from the corner of my eye that the man who was following me was Mr Charles Dickens. He carried in his left hand a paper cone from which he was extracting cherries. Some of these fruits he would eat, but every now and again he would silently put a cherry into the mouth of the child on my back. The child would suck the flesh and spit the stone onto the ground. When the paper cone was empty and the child was replete, Mr Dickens disappeared from view and as he did so, I heard him say, "Six o'clock. Just nice time to catch the Portsmouth train."'

This fragment was kept in a picture frame that hung in the parlour of the Palace Hotel in Copperfield. When The Best People built the replica of the Palace in the museum village, they were able to hang the original fragment in the parlour. Copies of the letter were sold in the village shops, along with other souvenirs and postcards.

Postcards

Many of the postcards were reproductions of old photographs that were tacked to the wall in the original Bluebird Café. They were pictures of miners, Aborigines, weddings, picnics, woodchops, shipwrecks, horses, houses, hotels and beautiful young women. The subjects of many of the photographs were children, often in their best clothes, sometimes in theatrical costume. A few were pictures of the children of miners, wearing simple, hand-me-down, home-made clothing.

You could learn a lot about old Copperfield from the back of the postcards The Best People made from the photographs:

'Temple of Eye of God'—Built by Philosopher Mean, this beautifully decorated temple was the meeting place for one of the many religious sects to grow up in rural Tasmania early this century. At the Temple, congregations were introduced to the beliefs, rituals and symbolism of a diversity of faiths. The wisdom and knowledge of Ancient Egypt can here be found alongside the gods and goddesses of Greece and the teachings of the Christian Church. A feature of the Temple was the collection of curiosities such as scrimshaw and fossils. One of the most interesting items in this collection was the Aboriginal skull which is believed to have belonged to William Lanney, known as King Billy, the last surviving male member of the race of Tasmanian Aborigines.'

'Palace Hotel'—Built by Philosopher Mean, the Palace, with its atmosphere of Edwardian luxury, was a centre of social and cultural life in the remote mountain area of Cape Grim. The ruby glass chandelier, made in India at the turn of the century, is one of the largest and most elaborate of its kind ever made. The original chandelier now hangs in the Fisher Museum in Chicago. The replica which hangs in the Palace Hotel of the Historic Museum Village was made in Italy in recent times, and has been exhibited in the Italian pavilion at Expo in Brisbane.'

'Charles Dickens Library'—Built by Philosopher Mean, this stone tower housed many thousands of books on subjects as diverse as the writings of Plato and instructions on how to make a beehive. Philosopher Mean's entire library is now housed in the Charles Dickens Library of the Historic Museum Village. It has recently been classified as a national treasure.'

'Bluebird Café'—Built by Philosopher Mean, this quaint, timber tea room, in its timeless style, was a haven for travellers as well as for local residents of Copperfield. *The Tried and Tested* recipe book had its humble beginnings here at the Bluebird when Eva Mean, niece of Philosopher, began collecting recipes which were later published in book form by the local Bedrock Press. Among the recipes are Hospitality Meringue Pie and Scripture Cake, for which the Bluebird was, in its heyday, justly famous. These dishes may be sampled at the Bluebird Café in the Historic Museum Village. Copies of *The Tried and Tested* may be purchased in the village gift shops.'

Bedrock

Bedrock Mean lives in the old Bluebird Café in the ghost town of Copperfield. She is the only human being for miles around. She stays there mourning for her daughter, hoping that one day Lovelygod will come back. Sometimes, not very often, people come to visit Bedrock. They are strangers who want to understand the spirit of the ghost town where the copper ran out and the child vanished from the face of the earth. Often Bedrock will not speak to the people who come there, but when she chooses to reply to the questions, she tells of her life in Copperfield, revealing a Copperfield that can never be known in the Historic Museum Village.

'One day,' she says, 'when Carrillo and I were about seven we cleaned the windows of the Bluebird. Eva gave us two shillings each. Then the glass was so clean and the sun was so bright that a small bird mistook the reflection of the world for the world itself and attempted to fly into what it thought it saw. The bird, I should have said, was a firetail with fine red feathers under its tail and on its head. It hit the glass and fell to the ground. Then it staggered around in front of the café until it toppled over on the doorstep. Carrillo got a biscuit tin and we put the bird in it. Later on the bird recovered and flew away.'

The upstairs window of the Bluebird Café reflects only the sky. Above this window the gable rises to a point on top of which is a spindle of turned wood painted blue. If you look up at the spindle and half close your eyes, especially at dusk, the spindle looks like a woman.

'We used to play in my grandfather's library,' Bedrock says. 'It could have been a lighthouse or a hollow tree or a very deep well. I imagined I could see a girl falling slowly past the shelves. We had a picture of Alice falling down the well, past the books, reaching out for a jar of marmalade. And a picture of Charles Dickens. It was the Charles Dickens Library. In the picture, Charles Dickens is sitting in a chair. His eyes are almost closed, but he can just see a girl who is no bigger than his hand. She's sitting on his knee. Figures of people from his books hover in the air behind him and above him. Some of these people emerge from blue clouds and are tinged with colour, but most of them are sketched in black and white with faint sepia shadows. The writer is in his library, his feet in his slippers resting on his footstool. He's got his desk in front of him, and on a table behind him there's an unlit lamp. The strongest light is coming through the window above the desk, and in this light, as if projected on a screen, float the figures of several women.'

'You know the picture by heart,' someone says.

'I used to like to stare at it. I suppose it is printed on my brain like a photograph. They took the picture to Launceston when they took the books. Now when I see it in my mind's eye I can imagine my daughter floating in through the window on the shaft of light.'

Bedrock seldom speaks of her daughter to strangers, and very rarely uses the child's name. When she does so her visitors are inclined to be embarrassed, for although the mystery of Lovelygod is the true reason for their visit, the mention of her name is shocking when it comes from the lips of her mother. Journalists have long since given up on the story of Lovelygod, and so Bedrock's rare visitors are not professional investigators determined to expose the truth, but amateur stickybeaks who have travelled up into the wild country along the Welcome River because they have seen the wax figure of Lovelygod in the waxworks at the Historic Museum Village, and have read there some of her story.

The wax figure is only two feet tall.

'What is this, a midget?' people say to the attendant.

'Yes,' he says, 'Lovelygod was one of the little people. She was ten years old when she disappeared, and she was only two feet high.'

Beneath the figure of Lovelygod is a notice: 'Lovelygod Mean, midget, born 1960, disappeared 1970. The mystery of her disappearance remains unsolved. Because of her deformity this child led a life of isolation and secrecy with her family in Copperfield. She disappeared in the night, leaving no trace. The police as well as the general public were completely baffled, and Lovelygod's family have consulted experts from all parts of the world—astrologers, hypnotists, soothsayers, faith-healers, priests, witches, wizards, dreamers and poets. Every possible theory has been proposed: she was stolen by scientists; she was murdered by her parents; she was taken by a Tasmanian devil; she was kidnapped by circus dealers, by priests, by the owner of a brothel; she wandered into the bush and fell through the floor of the horizontal forest; she was taken by creatures from outer space; she spontaneously combusted; she ran away. Did Lovelygod Mean ever really exist? Visitors are invited to register their theory of the disappearance by writing a brief account in the book provided.'

People write down their bizarre ideas about what could have happened, and then they move on to look at the other waxworks that stand in glass cases from old museums. There are life-size figures of miners and their families: the Means from the Palace Hotel; the O'Days who ran the mine; the Fishers; and even Nancy Best herself, for Nancy made several visits to the old town of Copperfield in the fifties. One large glass case contains Aborigines; another contains bushrangers; another Tasmanian devils and tigers. Stuffed birds sit in the branches of imitation trees; and wallabies, bandicoots and possums peer shyly from beneath the imitations of bushes. The skeleton of Truganini has been reproduced in fibreglass. It stands beside a lifelike statue of Truganini. The skull of William Lanney is said to be genuine.

Sometimes people who have bought postcards at the Museum Village take their postcards to Copperfield. A woman hands a card to Bedrock saying, 'Look, this is you and your brother.' It is a picture of a young woman standing behind a pram that contains the beaming, round baby forms of Bedrock and Carrillo. The title of the picture is 'Feeding the Swans'. No swans are to be seen. They must remain forever outside the frame of the photograph on their lake or their river or their ornamental pond. Like two bears in white frills the babies smile at the camera. The pram, like a wicker boat, holds the children safe.

'I remember the pleasure of riding in the pram,' Bedrock says. 'One day when we were parked in it next to the kiosk at the beach, a stranger came up and bought us an ice-cream in a square cone. The man who sold the ice-creams pushed a kind of double spade into the ice-cream so that a slab of it was caught between two plates of metal. Then he put the spade right into the cone, pressed a lever on the handle, and pulled the spade out of the cone, leaving the ice-cream inside it.

'Strangers were always staring at us because we were twins, and because of our curly red hair. We invented our own language, which was called Meaning and so people never knew what we were saying. In this way we have sometimes been able to protect ourselves from ridicule and cruelty.'

Bedrock tells these tales with quiet authority and gentle courtesy.

'She talked about ice-cream all the time,' they say. 'I wonder why she talked about ice-cream?'

Sometimes a bold busybody doing good says, 'Ms Mean, your

daughter has been missing for twenty years. Will you never give up hope?' When Bedrock chooses to answer such a question, she says, 'As long as I live, and as long as Lovelygod is missing, I will never give up hope. When I was a child I used to go past a haberdashery shop in Devonport, and in the window there was a pair of red shoes, a child's pink smocked dress, and a white satin ribbon tied in a bow. Next to these things was a tinted photograph of a five-year-old girl and a handwritten notice that told you Shirley Thompson set off one day all by herself to visit her grandmother who lived two streets away. Between Shirley's house and her grandmother's house, Shirley vanished, leaving no trace. As far as I know she has never been found. Her mother put the photo and the clothes, which were the same as the clothes Shirley had been wearing, in the window of the shop in the hope that somebody who knew something would see them. I remember being told that Mrs Thompson kept Shirley's room exactly as she would have kept it if Shirley had been there. And in the front window of the house she always left a light on for Shirley. I didn't understand it then, but now I know that the hope is unending because the guilt is unending. If Mrs Thompson had not let Shirley go out by herself, Shirley would not have disappeared. If Lovelygod had not been sleeping in the sunroom at the end of the Palace verandah with the windows wide open she would be here today. The mistake was mine; the guilt is mine; I will never give up hope.'

'Your brother has devoted much of his life to the search for Lovelygod. Where is he now?'

'I never know exactly where Carrillo is, but I know he will never give up hope, and when he finds her he will come home. They will come home.'

The Bluebird Café where Bedrock lives is an old building. The paint on the blue spindle is faded and flaking, but the spindle will still look like a woman if you squint up at it in the half light. Opposite the Bluebird is the crumbling mansion of soft red bricks where Brendan O'Day, manager of the mine, and his family used to live. The face of an ornamental griffin can be seen peering from a tangle of creepers that are weaving a green veil across the roof as the forest reaches out to reclaim the landscape. Rust dribbles down the white lace surfaces of the wrought iron on the verandahs; the front door is open, but not in welcome. Forlorn and despairing the windows are black and jagged holes where spiders thread their own dusty tapestries. Wild orchids grow in the garden where once were rows of marigolds and lavender. The roses in the sunken terrace have joined the ferns and brambles of the forest and now bloom high up in the branches of the trees. One side of the house is dominated by a gigantic rhododendron that blazes with a profusion of scarlet flowers.

The Palace Hotel has the traditional shape of an Australian hotel at the end of the nineteenth century. It has two storeys, verandahs, wrought iron and long, elegant windows. Somebody has removed all the doors and all the window frames so that the Palace has a blind and moaning look. The sunroom at the end of the verandah, Lovelygod's sunroom, is now a mound of dark green twisted vines that have worked together with a wisteria to produce a kind of natural basket.

The general store has disappeared beneath the encroaching forest. Locked inside the matted thatch of fern and creeper must be the remains of the stock. There would be knives and axes and rope, boots and brooms and cooking pots. Rats, mice and insects scuttle through the barley sugar, cinnamon rock, oil of cloves for toothache, tonics for the blood and lotions for the skin, the hair. They romp through sago, tobacco, rice, tea, flour, sugar, cheese, honey, jam, silk stockings, umbrellas, straw hats and bolts of calico.

Long ago, before the forest came and cloaked the store in green, one of the greatest pleasures of the people of Copperfield was to go to the store for supplies and a talk. Inside the shop was a special kind of smell. It was tantalizing, sweet, salty and distant. It was leather, crushed roses, herbs, and spice flitting through the gloom of the shop, leaving only a feeling of great age and time. In the general store, images would rise in the mind—images of stored fruit, of bones, feathers, pine trees, dust. You would think of the sea and the sand and the song of the wind on the water; the mark of the swallow's wing as it slices the air above the fields of wheat.

The Temple of the Eye of God has been cloaked by the forest, submerged beneath the thickening mantle of green.

In the Historic Museum Village the Best People have created a lifelike forest that is a tangle of myrtle, sassafras and tree-fern. White stars of the leatherwood and red sceptres of the waratah splash across the dark greens of the leaves. Monstrous grasses with strange heads loom up in heavy clumps, and long pink and crimson bells hang overhead on loops of ropey vine. Lips of toadstools, scarlet as pomegranates, glow in the damp, muffled places around the roots of trees. At the foot of a steep hillside into which has been carved five hundred steps, in a clearing beside a river, is the Temple of the Eye of God.

The temple is in the shape of a pyramid, constructed with timber and lined with the skins of wallabies. It is large enough to hold perhaps ten people. The walls are white, and painted on them in bright colours are pictures of snakes and soaring birds, fleshy flowers and goddesses with breasts like loaves of golden bread. At the apex of the arrangement of these pictures is a painting of the Eye of God. Inside the temple hangs a large triangular mirror around the edge of which is written in gold letters:

> The universe is the mirror of God;
> Man is the mirror of the universe.

Philosopher Mean's collection of curiosities has been brought from the original temple to the temple in the Museum Village. The collection includes a pair of spectacles that once belonged to Sarah Bernhardt, a lock of Matthew Brady's hair, a two-headed seahorse, Lewis Carroll's walking stick, fossils, shells, skeletons, and a phial of mud from Lourdes. William Lanney's skull is here.

William Lanney, known as King Billy, was considered to be the last of the full-blooded male Aborigines in Tasmania. He died at the Dog & Partridge in Hobart in 1869. They took his body to the morgue and put him next to the body of a schoolmaster. Rival groups of scientists tried to get possession of William's body for research. In the end he was buried without his hands, his feet, or his head. The schoolmaster's head was severed and had been placed on William's neck. The skin of William's face was drawn like a glove over the face of the other man. The hands and feet were later found, and from a portion of the skin one of the scientists made a pouch for his tobacco. Scientists and anthropologists searched for many years for the skull because they thought it would provide a link between mankind and the lesser animals. They never found it.

At the Palace Hotel in Queenstown, Abijah Mean gave a bottle of brandy to a sailor in exchange for the skull which the sailor claimed was the skull of King Billy.

William Lanney was buried according to the rites of the Church of England. His coffin was draped with the Union Jack, on top of which were placed bunches of wildflowers and the skin of one small possum.

When the Tasmanian Aborigines buried their dead, they made use of fire, which is sacred and purifying. They had no tools for digging deep graves, and so when a body was reduced to ash and bone they placed the remains in a circular hole in the earth. This hole was about eighteen inches wide, ten inches deep, and was covered over with a thick matting of grasses which were held in place by eight twigs like the spokes of a wheel, each twig being anchored by a stone. Above this structure was built a bark wigwam which had no doorway. These monuments were set in beautiful, beloved places on tops of gentle hills on the banks of streams. Such places were believed to be holy and sacred.

'Your daughter's statue in the waxworks makes her look a bit Aboriginal. Is that what she really looked like?' they say to Bedrock. And then they say, 'Her skin was pale; her hair was red; her features were Aboriginal. Is that right?'

'One of Lovelygod's forebears was an Aboriginal woman called Little Nell. She was my great-grandmother,' Bedrock says, 'the wife of Tobias Mean. Her family came from the Cape Portland tribe on the north-east coast.'

British colonists often gave Aboriginal people names from the books of Charles Dickens. William Lanney's brother, for instance, was called Barnaby Rudge. He had red hair and was simple-minded, like the original Barnaby whose face was 'strangely lighted up by something that was not intellect'.

Barnaby Rudge and William Lanney were two of the children of John Lanna and Nabrunga. This family lived in isolation in the hills behind Cape Grim from 1836 until 1841. They had refused to be relocated by the colonists when most Aborigines were sent to Flinders Island. They stole food from store huts belonging to the Van Diemen's Land Company. They lived in this way for five years, but finally, saying they were 'lonely', they agreed to be resettled. The official report of this occasion describes the family as 'coming forward' and as 'giving themselves up'. Having made this gesture of helplessness and hopelessness, they were 'relocated' to Flinders Island, and by 1847 all of them except William and Barnaby were dead.

Barnaby Rudge died at Oyster Cove in the far south-east of the island some time between 1847 and 1851. Named, surely, in cruel jest, he could have been no more than seventeen when he 'gave himself up' completely in the dismal, rotting colony on the far south coast of the Great South Land.

The traces left on the land by Barnaby Rudge, William Lanney and all their people were slight, scarcely more than they would leave if they were fish moving through the water, or birds through the air.

Bedrock's inquisitors say, 'Is it true you and your brother invented a religion as well as a language?'

'It was one of our games.'

'A peculiar sort of game if you ask me.'

Bedrock remembers the game, but she doesn't answer the visitor.

I remember one afternoon when we were sitting here in the Bluebird. It was raining (it often rained) and we were copying things from the Bible into an exercise book. We made a list with the help of a concordance of biblical quotations that contained the word 'pool'. An angel went down at a certain season into the pool and troubled the water. We weren't inventing a religion. But I think we believed we were. Our grandfather was always talking about this religion or that religion. I imagined the great multitudes of impotent folk at the pool of Bethesda. Impotent folk, blind, halt, and withered waiting for the moving of the water. They wait for an angel to come and trouble the water. The first one to get into the water will be cured. We imagined getting everyone, all the multitudes of impotent folk, to go to the Pool of Bethesda at Cradle Mountain. We would arrange fake miracles. You would have different kinds of miracles in different places. You could cure blind people at Damascus Gate, mad people at Solomon's Jewels, and lame people at the Walls of Jerusalem. We made lists of all the places in Tasmania where you could expect to stage miracles: Paradise, the Promised Land, Bagdad, Jericho, Dove Lake. Ours was a religion of miracles. The miracles were fakes. Because of our grandfather's interest in the world's religions, and the existence of the Temple of the Eye of God, Carrillo and I could think of nothing to believe in. Nothing, that is, except a kind of magic. We hoped for magic, for miracles, but we knew that if we wanted to show miracles to people, we would have to fake them. Our religion never got beyond a theoretical stage. We planned miracles but we never got round to demonstrating them. Tilly the barmaid was interested in being a part of the performance. She was very fat and suffered from asthma, and we were going to put on a show where we pretended that her asthma had been cured, at least temporarily. But she started having such serious attacks she had to leave the hotel and go to Launceston for treatment. So we never did our miracle.

I used to think Tilly was fascinating, even beautiful, in a strange way, until the day I saw her in the bath. She had left the bathroom door unlocked, and I went in, and there was Tilly in the water. Her hair was up in a topknot and she completely filled the bath. Her skin was stretched and blotchy like sausages. She sat up when she saw me and a wave of soapy water sloshed onto the floor. Her library book fell into the water, and the thing she held against me was that the book was ruined and she couldn't finish it. She lived for her library books that came up on the train in parcels for her every month.

'My sister belongs to a book club in Launceston,' Tilly told me.

'Her sister pinches books from the public library,' the chamber-maid said.

'I get so bored on my days off,' Tilly said, ignoring her, 'when there's nothing to read.'

'Is it true,' Bedrock's inquisitors say, 'that they once found the skeleton of a rhinoceros in the swamp behind Smithton?'

'Yes, it was a marsupial rhinoceros named *Nototherium mitchelli*. You could go and see the skeleton in the main hall of the Royal Society in Hobart.'

The oldest branch of the Royal Society outside the British Isles was in Hobart, and the skeleton of the rhinoceros was there, as well as a display of statues of Aborigines around a campfire and the skeleton of Truganini. All this has been faithfully reproduced by The Best People in the Historic Museum Village.

'Have you ever seen a Tasmanian tiger?' they ask Bedrock. Some people have imagined Lovelygod could have been taken by a thylacine. 'Do you believe they are extinct?'

'I have never seen one. When my father was a child he went to the Hobart zoo and there he saw the animal believed to be the last of the thylacines.'

Phoenix Mean was not filled with fear when he saw this animal, called a tiger. And he was not filled with awe, but pity. He held on to the outside bars of the rusty cage in which was a sad old tiger. He stared at the animal for a long time because it looked so dusty and so small and so unfierce, and because it was the last. He was looking at the last one of these in the whole world. Many people passed by as he stood gripping the bars of the cage. Phoenix heard the chirrup of the voices of the little girls, the babble of the babies, shouts of boys. He overheard a man say, 'Dying out. They're dying out.' Children in woollen overcoats with velvet collars glanced at the animal in the cage and said, 'Dying out.'

Like an echo in a valley or a ripple on the surface of a pond, the animal was dying out.

At about the time when Bedrock and Carrillo were planning to stage their miracles, Nancy Best was exploring Tasmania looking for suitable places to put caravan parks. She went to Copperfield. As she drove in from the coast, through the Back Woods, she had the feeling that eyes were watching her in the silent darkness of the forest. In her imagination the Back Woods were inhabited by lurking lunatics, murderers, miners, sawmillers, hermits, bee farmers. She fancied she would meet inarticulate, hairy children scuttling on all fours.

Nancy stayed at the Palace Hotel, finding out all she could about Copperfield and the surrounding country, and taking hundreds of photographs. There was nowhere here, she thought, that you could put a caravan park. She talked to everybody, including the children, gathering information which she would use years later when she reproduced this place. She gave Bedrock a bottle of perfume. She let Bedrock sit on her bed while she made up her face. She would stretch her eyebrow between two fingers and pluck the hairs out with tweezers. Then she would draw a line on her skin with a soft, black pencil. Bedrock would sit on the bed and look into the mirror where she could see herself as well as Nancy, and a section of the room.

When Nancy had gone, Bedrock had the job of putting fresh sheets on the bed in Nancy's room. Under the bed Bedrock found a page of a letter in Nancy's handwriting. She read the letter. When she did this she felt as if some evil truth had come alive in her hand. Nancy had befriended Bedrock and Carrillo and their family, but in the letter she wrote, 'I am stuck in the bush now, in the absolute back of beyond. This is real hill-billy country with things you would never believe. I know you will tell me I imagined all this. They have a crackpot religion for one thing, where they worship the skulls of Aborigines. And one day I went into this sort of lighthouse out the back of the pub (we're miles from the sea, you realize), and it (I mean the lighthouse) was full of rare books. Most of the people here are very sly. And I have been driven completely mad by a gang of stickybeak, show-off children. The place has great possibilities, but we'll have to have a good think about how we could use it. I should have said that the people here have weird made-up names such as Phoenix and Bedrock (!) and God knows what else.'

Bedrock read the page of the letter. She stared at it and then she tore it into fragments and squashed the whole lot into a hard little ball in her hand. She left the linen from the bed on the floor of the hallway and stood on the landing for a long time, gazing at a window of coloured glass. She went slowly down the stairs, feeling the bannister, looking down at the carpet runner, following the pattern with her gaze. The ball of Nancy's letter was tight inside her fist. She headed for the parlour where she could throw the letter on the fire.

The parlour was a red room in which a fire was always burning. The room glowed with a soft red light that was shed by clusters of red glass lamps. In the daytime during the week not many people used the parlour. This day the only people in there were a young man and woman who held hands across a table and stared into each other's eyes. They paid no attention to Bedrock as she came in and stood by the fireplace, squeezing the letter between both hands.

Bedrock looked into the fire in confused rage and sadness. She kept trying not to think the words of the letter, but they came back to her like mocking imps: crackpot religion and stickybeak show-offs.

For a moment the room was as still as a painting in thick, dark oils in many shades of glowing red. A young man in a brown jacket was looking into the eyes of a girl in burgundy velvet. The couple were sitting at a table by the piano over which hung an embroidered shawl. A dog was asleep on the hearth, and a fire was burning in the grate. Next to the fireplace stood a girl in a white apron. She was about to cast a ball of paper into the flames.

'No,' Nancy said when she got home from Copperfield the day Bedrock burned the letter, 'no, you definitely couldn't put a caravan park up there. The road's bad going in from the coast, and the country's too wild. Hill-Billy Holidays is one thing. But Copperfield is off the map as far as I'm concerned.' It was forty years later that Nancy saw her new Copperfield being built on Cataract Hill. Echoing Nancy's words from the past, the Mayor of Launceston said in a speech as he was about to set off on a flight in a Fly-By-Nite helicopter to look at the work in progress on the Hill, 'This will put Tasmania on the map once and for all.' The City Council, the Tasmanian Government, and the Trevallyn Progress Association worked together on the project of the Historic Museum Village, and the Mayor, the Premier, and the President of the Progress Association could often be seen in a Fly-By-Nite or, if it was daytime, a Dragonfly, checking on the building. They decided to commission a playwright to write a play inspired by the new Copperfield.

'What playwrights have we got?' the Premier said.

'You mean Tasmanian?' the Mayor asked.

'Preferably.'

'Well, none that I know of living here. But there would be some overseas, or probably over the other side.'

'It'd be good if we could get one that had some connection or other with Copperfield. Or Trevallyn.'

'Or both.'

'Both would be fantastic.'

'Both is too much to hope for.'

But both, as it turned out, was not too much to hope for. They contacted the Australian Society of Authors and learned of the existence of Virginia O'Day.

Virginia O'Day

Virginia was described in the letter the Society of Authors sent to the Mayor of Launceston as 'an expatriate Tasmanian play-wright and novelist living in Massachusetts. She grew up in the picturesque Launceston suburb of Trevallyn. She began writing fiction when she was eighteen years old, during a holiday spent in the mining town of Copperfield in the north-west of Tasmania. Her play *The Bluebird Café Murders* has enjoyed considerable success in the West End and on Broadway. O'Day's other plays include *Brendan the Navigator* and the musical comedy *Runaway Jane*. Her best-known novel is the epic *Wild Lavender*, and her other novels include the works *A* and *B*. She has written a collection of essays titled *Photography in Fiction*; an analysis of exploration in the Pacific titled *Who Made History Where*; and a textbook on the writing of fiction, *The Low Brown Writer's Notebook*.'

They found an old photograph of Virginia in the archives of the Launceston *Examiner*. It showed Virginia surrounded by her collection of snow domes when she was twelve years old. Here she was described as 'eldest daughter of ear, nose and throat surgeon Dr Vincent O'Day and Mrs O'Day, with her collection of snow domes. "I collect snow domes because they are not as flat as stamps," Virginia said. She spends much of her spare time dusting the domes and re-arranging them. They have come from all over the world, and some of the examples in

Virginia's collection are rare and valuable.'

Virginia was the first child of Margaret and Vincent O'Day. She was born in the conservatory of the O'Day's house in Trevallyn on 10 August 1933. They took all the plants out of the conservatory and scrubbed the floor and draped the benches with sheets so that beautiful little Margaret O'Day could have the baby there. With the birth of each of her children (and there were seven of them) Margaret O'Day put on more weight so that she became, in the end, enormously fat. Her eldest daughter, Virginia, on the other hand, decided to stop eating at the age of seventeen and became very, very thin. The sight of Virginia and her mother together was, because of the family resemblance and the difference in size, comic. By the time Virginia was seventeen, the conservatory where she had been born was being used as a storeroom for rusty bicycles, half empty tins of paint, and sections of old fences and gates. The plants had long since died in their pots, and the glass walls were blurred with dirt and spider webs. Children had written on the glass with their fingers. On the marble floor, someone had drawn a picture of Mickey Mouse with coloured chalks. And with an indelible pencil a child had written over and over in bright purple on the marble floor: 'Virginia stinks'.

Events Leading to Virginia's Visit to Copperfield

Eva Mean took Bedrock and Carrillo, her niece and nephew, to Launceston for a holiday to stay with the O'Days in 1950. The children were ten years old and had never been so far away from home without their mother before. They travelled by train and had sandwiches and cake and Swiss roll and thermoses of tea. Dr O'Day met them at the station (which was not far from where Nancy Best lived when she was young) and drove them through the city, across the river, and up the hillside of Trevallyn to the house. When they were crossing the Tamar, Dr O'Day said to look to the left. Far below they could see yellowy water frothing between dark hillsides. This was the Gorge. The hillside was covered with trees through which could be seen parts of houses. At the gate of the O'Day's house was a walnut tree, and Rosie, Virginia's younger sister, was sitting in the branches. She was holding a bunch of flowers she had picked for Eva.

Rosie jumped down from the walnut tree and landed in long grass. The visitors came towards her in a procession with Dr O'Day coming last carrying the suitcases. He was smiling all the time, his big teeth showing in his round pink face. Rosie rushed up to Eva, thrusting the flowers at her with both hands, like a bridesmaid with a posy. She joined the procession and they all went up the brick path past garden beds full of yellow weeds, and grass with hens in it. The hens could scarcely be seen because the grass was so high. You could just see the tops of nursery chairs that had long ago been abandoned in the garden. A china doll lay sleeping in a wicker pram which was all but invisible in the grasses. You could imagine that strings of beads and lead soldiers and small wooden animals from Noah's Ark must litter the floor of this wild grass sea. Would a child be lost down there in the green labyrinth? The child is lost, hungry, weeping, calling for her mother.

Margaret O'Day came to the door and said, 'You're here.' She was wearing a floral apron and was fatter than Tilly the barmaid. A little girl with a dirty face was hiding behind her knee. Dr O'Day put the cases down in the hall which was full of gumboots and school blazers and hockey sticks and panama hats. Margaret O'Day kissed Eva and then she pressed Bedrock and Carrillo to her spongy bosom. The child with the dirty face pulled at her mother's skirt.

Bedrock stood staring stupidly at Margaret O'Day. She had always imagined Margaret would be glamorous. She would be a slender lady in a taffeta ball gown and a fur stole. She would go out with Dr O'Day to important receptions and dances, clapping politely after speeches, with dainty hands in white gloves to the elbows. She would meet the Queen. She would open flower shows, and small girls in white dresses would present her with posies of flowers as if she were the Queen herself.

The kitchen of the O'Day's house was huge and dark. It had a long table with benches at the sides and a chair at either end. One of these chairs was for Margaret and one was for the doctor. Everybody else pushed and wriggled onto the benches, supervised by Belinda who helped with the cooking and cleaning and washing, ironing and mending. The kitchen floor was black. The tablecloth was white and everybody had a serviette in a silver ring with a name on it. The small girl with the dirty face was called Doll. Bedrock was puzzled by this until she saw Doll's serviette ring which said 'Dolores'. Margaret dished out steak and kidney from a large brown pot. The plates were passed down the table and Rosie served out peas and potatoes. When she had finished she had to take a plate of food upstairs to Virginia.

'Virginia's my mad sister,' Rosie said to Bedrock and Carrillo. 'She's seventeen. Every night I take her supper up to her, but she never eats it. She never eats anything, you know.' She left the room with the tray. Two dogs lay under the table eating scraps of meat that the children passed to them. Pudding was bottled peaches and custard which Doll would not eat because she said she hated the lumps and the skin of the custard. 'Pretend it's pus,' Damien, one of her brothers said, and Doll screamed and ran out of the room.

'I wish you wouldn't upset her like that,' Margaret said. Damien ate Doll's pudding.

'I get the peaches from a patient in Perth,' Dr O'Day said. Bedrock thought that was a beautiful thing to be able to say and she thought she would write it in her diary when she went upstairs. She thought she would like to remember everything they had all said, and remember how everyone had looked as they sat around the table. She began to wish she had a camera. Then she realized she really wanted to *be* a camera. She wanted to be telescopes and microscopes and cameras. She imagined she was taking pictures of the knives and forks on the table. The knives had bone handles squared off at the ends and chipped at the edges; the forks were heavy silver ones and some of the prongs were bent.

Rosie came downstairs with Virginia's tray. Virginia had eaten nothing.

'What did I tell you,' Rosie said. 'She just lies on her bed with her face to the wall getting thinner and thinner every minute.' Then Rosie turned to her mother and said, 'Anyway, she might die.'

'No, dear,' Margaret said, 'there is no need to be afraid of that happening. She won't die.'

'Brenda Lacey died.'

'Brenda had a tumour.'

'On the brain. *And* only one kidney.' Rosie said this looking past her mother, past Bedrock, gazing out the window. 'Brenda wouldn't eat either. It was the same thing.'

'It was a different thing altogether,' her mother said. 'You mustn't worry like this, Rose.'

'It was practically the same thing anyway,' Rosie said. Her mother turned away. Rosie went on: 'See those tomatoes growing in the weeds in the garden. Well, they're Virginia's tomatoes. Do you want to know why Virginia grows tomatoes?'

'Rosie,' Margaret said, 'nobody wants to hear all that nonsense about the tomatoes.' But Rosie said, 'Michael Mullvaney died, and Mrs Mullvaney was Virginia's teacher and she told the girls they had to give up eating meat so they could offer up the sacrifice for Michael Mullvaney's soul in Purgatory. So Virginia gave up meat and then she decided to give up vegetables as well. She said she wouldn't eat anything that could be destroyed by her eating it. She said she was going to stop hurting things for the sake of Michael Mullvaney's soul in Purgatory. Then she got the idea that if she ate only tomatoes and the seeds went through her own body, if you see what I mean, and she ate the tomatoes that grew from the seeds, she wouldn't be hurting tomatoes.

Michael Mullvaney was riding his bike and hanging on to the back of a truck and the truck stopped suddenly and Michael was thrown into somebody's rock garden and killed. Then one day in Mrs Mullvaney's class the window was open and a dandelion fairy drifted in and Mrs Mullvaney said it was the spirit of Michael, her dead son. And she made all the girls kneel down there and then and say the rosary while the spirit of Michael Mullvaney sailed around the room and out the door. Virginia said they had to stop themselves from dying laughing, and they hoped he would fly into the inkwell.'

'That will be quite enough, Rosie,' Margaret said. Bedrock was sorry when Rosie stopped talking. When Margaret left the room Rosie said, 'They thought the idea about the dandelion fairy was mad, but Virginia and some of her friends took up the one about giving up food. It was Virginia who invented the bit about the tomatoes. Virginia's very bossy, and she bossed the other girls but their mothers put a stop to it and made them take up food again. But nobody can make Virginia. Whenever we offer her food she says we're trying to poison her. She'll die anyway. And she's got everything worked out—how the funeral has to be—and she's made a will with a description of the flowers and the music and prayers. What she's wearing. It says what she's wearing. I told you she was mad.'

'What's she wearing?' Bedrock said.

'Some kind of blue velvet princess outfit like in a pantomime. She says the dressmaker will do it between death and burial. Virginia said that's what dressmakers do. People put lipstick and powder on corpses. And a girl told Virginia if you stop eating for long enough your periods will stop. You just dry up. She hates getting her period so much she thought that was another good reason for not eating. It works. Virginia hasn't had a period for six months. And also not eating saves her from going to the university. My father wants her to go to Hobart to study to be a teacher. She'd make a good teacher, of course, being mad, but she hates the idea and said she'd rather be a nun in the desert or dead. What she has is an incurable condition. A man came over from the mainland who's a psychiatrist and he examined her and he told my father the only thing to do was cut out a part of her brain with a hot wire. Or else put her to sleep for about a year and hope she felt different when she woke up.'

Bedrock tried to imagine Virginia upstairs in her bed. She was thin and dying with her face to the wall. She had her hands over her ears to shut out the cries of the boys who were playing in the street behind the house. Princess Virginia lay on her couch in the tower. Her gown was velvet and in her hair she wore a coronet of pearls and rubies. She was as white as milk, wrapped in a silence where she could hear the breathing of moths. The light in her tower room was blue. A dreadful stillness was in that room, broken now and then when the princess sighed and stirred and picked up her quill to write a poem. She wrote about owls and yew trees and the moon.

'But she won't really die, will she?' Bedrock said.

'She might,' Rosie said.

'Then I'm frightened of sleeping in the room next to hers. She might die on the other side of the wall. I always sleep with Carrillo.'

'With your brother?'

'Why not?'

'Such a thing would not be tolerated,' Rosie said.

Rosie's bedroom which Bedrock shared was the only place Bedrock had seen in the house that was not cluttered with piles of books and shoes and toys and bundles of old clothes. The walls of the bedroom were covered with wallpaper that was decorated with bunches of violets. The beds had white quilts and the curtains were made from white lace.

'I keep everything in here,' Rosie said, and she opened the door of a large wardrobe. Books, comics, hats, sandals, toys, clothes and several kites came tumbling out. Rosie gave them all a push and quickly shut the door.

In the next room Virginia lay in her bed with her face to the wall, thinking of roast dinners and banana cake and tins of sardines. She imagined herself downstairs in the pantry. It was a large pantry lined with shelves painted green. On the top shelves Margaret O'Day kept rows and rows of glass jars containing preserved fruit. The shelf second from the top was for the supplies that had been brought up from the garden trench after the end of the Second World War. The trench was now a place where Dr O'Day stored old books, and where the children played. It was a deep, safe tunnel dug at the bottom of the back garden near the fowl house. The walls of the trench were lined with pale old maps of the world. The trench provisions that were now kept in the pantry in case of some other great emergency were tins of beef and tins of sardines and powdered milk and gentleman's relish and jam. Margaret sometimes wondered whether the contents of the tins would be fit to eat after all this time, but she just left them on the shelf anyway. The lower shelves had ordinary, everyday supplies and a certain amount of china and glassware. Virginia's mind roamed around the shelves of her mother's pantry, lingering over jars of peanut butter and glass bottles of Paris almonds.

'Did she leave you anything in her will?' Bedrock asked Rosie in the next room.

'Plenty,' Rosie said. 'She wants everybody to have her things so we can remember always how good and kind and beautiful she was and feel sorry. I'm getting her silver charm bracelet blessed by the Pope and her marquisite Scotty dog brooch with fake ruby eyes. I'm getting her musical box from Switzerland and her gold locket and the sewing basket that belonged to our aunt who was a nun and was killed in a bus crash in India. I'll get her brown velvet coat but I hate it, and half her snow domes. Damien gets the other half.'

Virginia banged on the wall with her fist and called out to the girls to shut up.

'I said she was bossy,' Rosie said.

'She doesn't sound like she's dying.'

'Don't worry. She won't die just yet because there's still a lot of food she doesn't want to eat, and a lot more bossing she wants to do. She's having fun, you know.'

'Shut up!' Virginia screamed from the next room.

Rosie fell asleep at once, but Bedrock lay awake in the strange bedroom. She was lonely and frightened by her loneliness. She heard through the wall a moaning and then a screaming. The house was suddenly awake and filled with light and people running and calling. Rosie woke up and went out to see what was going on. When she went back to bed she told Bedrock what had happened. A cockroach had crawled into Virginia's ear. Using an instrument with tiny metal claws on the end, Dr O'Day had crushed the insect and removed it from Virginia's ear in sections.

'And once,' Rosie said to Bedrock, 'my father took guess what out of a man's ear?'

'I can't guess,' Bedrock said.

'I'll give you a clue. The man was a diver.'

'Seaweed?' Bedrock said.

'Seaweed? No, of course not. It was a crayfish. A tiny baby crayfish that got into this man's ear and my father got it out in pieces.'

'How could that happen?'

'If you don't believe me, ask my father. The man had been deaf for weeks and just about dying from the pain. After Daddy got the crayfish out, the man (he was Italian) threw his arms around my father and kissed him with tears running down his face. I know of many more unusual cases if you want to hear about them. I wish Virginia would shut up now.'

They put their heads under the covers to muffle the sound of Virginia's moaning.

'She'll go to any lengths to get attention, you know.'

'It's lucky your father was a doctor for ears.'

'Just pity the poor cockroach.'

Bedrock tried to think about other things. She thought about all the pictures on the wall of the Bluebird Café at home. The images in the photographs faded with the passing of time so that some of the oldest pictures were very faint. The surfaces of the paper had in some cases been eaten by silverfish and so the words written on the backs of the photographs had disappeared. Some of the pictures had been partly nibbled away. A bride stood next to a bridegroom who was absent except for his shoes and part of one arm. Bedrock fell asleep.

The next day they all went to the Gorge. The water known as the Gorge divides two hillsides, one of which is called the wet hill and the other the dry hill. The O'Day's house was on the wet hill. Round the side of the hill, thirty feet up from the water was a path that led to a glade where leafy, English trees shaded sloping lawns. Peacocks walked on the lawns, and under the trees was a rustic tea room and an elegant Edwardian bandstand.

Everyone except Virginia went to the Gorge for a picnic. They walked down to the bridge where they turned off at the path. They carried picnic things—rugs, cushions, hats, baskets of food. The child Doll was in a shabby striped pusher that was too small for her. She looked like an orphan, with bare feet and a runny nose, although she was wearing a white frilly sunbonnet starched and ironed that morning by Belinda.

At the entrance to the path was a turnstile where Dr O'Day put money in and everyone passed through. Dr O'Day was carrying his camera and he kept taking pictures. The caretaker of the Gorge lived in a house that looked like a witch's house. It was almost concealed by bushes and vines and could be reached only by climbing a narrow wooden staircase that zigzagged up the side of the hill. The cliff towered darkly above the straggly line of people; the rocks jutted from the dark growth of ferns and creeping plants. To the left of the path was a railing from which the cliff fell away down to the water. The dry hill was brown and barren with only a few native trees growing on it.

Someone had tried to grow an apple tree on the dry hill, but the apple tree was stunted and covered with dust. Into the faces of the rocks along the path on the wet hillside were scratched the names of people and drawings of hearts and arrows. Some of the rocks by the side of the path formed caves, and the walls of the caves were covered with writing. 'Done by larrikins,' Dr O'Day said, 'larrikins and vandals.' High up on the wall of one of the caves could be seen the words: 'A little girl was in this place'.

Dr O'Day had to shout to be heard above the roar of the water. Rosie cupped her hand to Bedrock's ear and whispered, 'He doesn't know Virginia wrote the one about the little girl.' Then Rosie shouted, 'People jump over the Gorge and drown.' And her father shouted, 'That will be enough of that, Rose.'

The first thing people imagined, when they passed through the turnstile and fell into the shadow of the hill where no sunlight ever shone on the sullen man-ferns and the seeping stones, was rushing to the railing and jumping into the air above the water that foamed and swirled and roared below.

The picnic party walked in the cool darkness of the path that wound along the cliff towards the distant clearing. The boys ran ahead, swinging every now and then on the railing, calling across to the dry hill to get an echo. Rosie said a tribe of Aborigines used to live on the hillside. She said they left some drawings in the caves, but nobody could tell any more which drawings they were. A bushranger, she said, was found dead in one of the caves. He died of starvation even though he had already eaten two other bushrangers and also somebody's baby.

In the clearing, flowers in bright clumps grew in flower beds around the edges of the lawns. There must once have been a gardener with an axe and a leather pouch full of acorns. He pushed his way along the cliff before the path was made. He came at last to this place where he began to chop down some of the trees. He took the acorns out of the pouch and pushed them into the ground, scratching up the earth and patting it down

again. When he had finished, he sat on a rock in the shade
and took a salt-beef sandwich from the pocket of his jacket.
He fetched water from a nearby spring. Birds, forest creatures,
bushrangers and Aborigines watched him from the thick darkness of the bushes. He picked up his axe and went back the way
he had come.

That night he sat in his hut and wrote by the light of a candle:
'Today I made my way through the damp and sombre foliage
of the forest beside the cataract. In mid-afternoon I reached a
place where the vegetation was thinner, where some light pen-
etrated the umbrella of mountain laurel, myrtle, blackwood,
dogwood, and sassafras. After felling a number of smaller trees,
I planted, as was my intention, some of the acorns which I have
carried with me from my home in Surrey. Now that I have made
this initial exploration of the land beside the cataract, I plan to
return and set up camp there, and I will clear away the trees
which grow there and supplant them with the oaks and elms of
England. I will make in there a place of gentle lawns and shady
walks where families in years to come will spend pleasant after-
noons beneath the trees, and where musicians will play to the
delight of children, lovers, and old men.'

When this man returned to the cataract he found the process
of clearing the land was slower than he had hoped. He chopped
a circle of bark from around the circumference of some of the
stubborn trees and left them to die. They died, and in their
place grew spreading oaks and elms above the sloping lawns.

On the day of the picnic the O'Day family finally sat under
one of the oak trees near the tea room. The people under the
next tree were the Quinlans who lived in the house nextdoor
to the O'Days. Mr Quinlan was the pharmacist who had made
up the drops for Virginia's ear. Behind the tea room was a gravel
path leading off into dark woods where daffodils and bluebells
grew in the spring, and where rhododendrons had been thickly
planted under the trees. The paths and flower beds were edged
with iron loops painted green. Peacocks moved in slow silence

across the lawns, never displaying their tails, but letting them sweep the ground behind them. The picnic food was sandwiches wrapped in lettuce leaves to keep them fresh, and chocolate cake and ginger beer. When everyone had eaten, and the children had run round and round the rotunda meant for bands on special occasions, the Quinlans and the O'Days went for a walk to the suspension bridge.

The suspension bridge was a very long, narrow footbridge that hung high above the water. The water twisted and roared and frothed beneath the bridge, and the bridge looked as fragile as a cat's cradle. Margaret O'Day and Mary Quinlan talked, as they always talked, about ordinary everyday things. The silverfish in the carpets and cupboards were like a plague. The old-fashioned remedies were still the best. Cloves and salt sprinkled in dark places; a small glass half-filled with flour and left inside a cupboard as a trap. You could try painting the insides of cupboards with oil of cedar, although some people swore that the silverfish took oil of cedar as an open invitation.

In single file the two families started to cross the bridge, and the bridge began to sway. Bedrock imagined that when fat Margaret and fat Mary got into the middle of the bridge it would snap and they would all be tossed like jelly babies into the distant, creamy, frothy water.

When they had all crossed the bridge and it was time to go back, Doll O'Day refused to go. People tried to persuade her. Her father said he would carry her. Bedrock imagined Doll twisting about in terror and flying off her father's back. She saw the flurry of Doll's yellow dress, the flash of her bare legs. Doll would spear the scummy bubbles, a tiny rubber doll far, far away down in the water. She would disappear, bob up for a split second, and then go down forever. They offered Doll an ice-cream at the tea room if she would cross the bridge. Her brothers threatened to kill her if she did not. She screamed and cried and would not cross.

Rosie and Bedrock were left on the bank with Doll. The

three girls watched as everyone filed across the suspension bridge like soldiers. They saw the bridge swaying like a ribbon in a storm. They saw all the Quinlans and all the O'Days and Carrillo and Eva and Belinda disappearing mysteriously into the trees on the other side. They played sadly in the dry grass on the hillside until Dr O'Day arrived in the car to collect them. Dr O'Day told them they were a sorry lot, and then he took a photograph of them standing next to the car.

'I'll call this one "Orphans of the Storm",' he said, and Rosie said, 'Daddy's hobby is photography. He gives most of the pictures a name.'

When Dr O'Day printed the photographs he took on the day of the picnic he was surprised by a trick of the light in one of them. It was a photograph of all the children, Quinlans and O'Days. The youngest Quinlan was Francis Xavier, known as FX. He was subnormal. But in the photograph FX looked perfectly ordinary whereas Doll looked quite half-witted. Vincent O'Day studied the print of the picture for a long time, wondering about the effects of the light, the truth of the suggestion in the picture, the meaning of the way in which the natures of Doll and FX seemed to have been transferred. He considered destroying the print and the negative. But this was a thing he never did. He filed, recorded and kept his negatives in boxes in the cellar, and he kept a copy of each print, and placed these copies in albums. So the normal FX and the idiot Doll went into the file as a negative and into the album as a print. Vincent wondered whether the photograph could be a true picture of the way things were. Was Doll an idiot? Was FX a perfectly normal child? Nobody ever commented on the print. Vincent thought, when he thought about it at all, that perhaps the whole thing was present only in his imagination.

Vincent O'Day sometimes wished he could take photographs of things that existed only in his imagination. He wished he could imagine so powerfully that the image in his mind would be manifest. He could then photograph it. He imagined a carousel with horses and music at the Gorge, just in front of the rotunda. The centre of the carousel is a maypole from which flutter ribbons. Some of the columns are made from twisted brass; some are crystal. Straight columns have been decorated with mosaics of bright stones. One carriage is shaped like a swan, another is a hare, another a lion. The painted horses have come from distant deserts and their eyes rage with fire; their brows are fringed with foam and milky moonlight. On the most beautiful horse sits the most beautiful woman.

While everyone was at the Gorge on the day of the picnic, Virginia was alone in the house. She liked the house when it was empty. She had a bath, admiring her ribcage and her shins. Almost no flesh was visible on her body. She examined the bones of her face in a small hand mirror, and was satisfied by the size of her eyes which looked enormous. Although she had eaten nothing that morning, she was still able to vomit when she pushed her fingers down her throat. She thought that one day she might begin to vomit her own insides. She put on a dress and her brown overcoat which she pulled in tight with the belt. Her shoes were too big. Like a long, brown animal Virginia slipped out the back door of the house and took a deep breath in the fresh air.

In her music satchel Virginia carried a large exercise book and her fountain pen. She was going up to the old Scotch cemetery to sit in one of the ruined sepulchres and write her novel. What if the family came home before she got back? She enjoyed the risk. So far she had never been caught when out on one of her excursions. Sometimes she went to the museum which was a still, silent, weird place smelling of dust. Virginia would wander around among the stuffed animals and Egyptian mummies and Chinese gods. Sometimes she went to the public library which was old and dark and where she sat reading in the shadows. She imagined people didn't know who she was. On the day of the picnic she got on a bus and went to the cemetery.

The old Scotch cemetery was a ruin on the side of one of the hills of the town. From the hillside could be seen lower hills, the valley, the centre of the town, the river, and, in the distance, the hill where Virginia lived. In the cemetery were the remains of the graves of Scottish settlers who came to the island in the nineteenth century. Many of the graves were sepulchres cut like caves into the clay of the hillside. Doors like prison bars hung open on rusty hinges; and broken pieces of grave furniture lay scattered in piles of rubble on the ground. Any treasures that might have been placed in the graves had long since gone, for the cemetery had been looted and laid bare. Robbers had been; gipsies had camped there; now children, forbidden by their parents to do so, came there to play. Or they came as Virginia came, to dream and lose themselves in morbid romance. Ghosts, bushrangers, murderers, witches, kidnappers, nymphs, angels, gods and lovers lived in the sepulchres. A fierce tribe of Aborigines lurked behind the rocks of the hillside.

Virginia sat in the doorway of a sepulchre with her notebook and pen. She used green ink. Before she began writing she spent some time looking down into the valley where a mist was still hanging. She could see the Chinese market-gardener working in his garden, moving up and down the rows of vegetables, watering and weeding. The man was so small in the distance that he resembled, in his basket hat, a figure in a porcelain statue. Virginia imagined she was a princess sitting on a soft green hillside, watching her Chinese slave working in her flower garden. She is wearing her blue silk dress, and on her knee she has a letter from her lover who lives beyond the mountains. He will come to her at midnight on the hillside; he has sent her bunches of white violets which lie carelessly at her feet. At her feet, the violets. Hidden in the hill behind her, rats.

Virginia was writing an historical romance called *Savage Paradise*. The hero was David Macintosh, the heroine Elizabeth Scott. They both came from Scotland, he from Glasgow, she from the Isle of Skye. They met in Van Diemen's Land. After a long and troubled romance, they married and became the owners of whole mountains, taming the waters, and fighting off marauding bushrangers and blacks.

Virginia thought of her family at the Gorge. They would be eating cake and making useless conversation with the Quinlans. Her father would be running round taking photographs. They would be drinking ginger beer. Virginia preferred to drink water from public taps, and to find scraps of food in rubbish tins. She imagined that her mother's food would poison or choke her, but she ate apple cores and dry crusts from rubbish tins with greed. She wrote in her notebook with her green ink until she got too cold to stay in the graveyard, and she went home. She arrived at the front gate of the house as her father was driving out to collect the three children left at the end of the suspension bridge.

'You will come with me,' Dr O'Day said to Virginia. She sat next to him during the drive to and from the bridge, but she would not speak. She would explain nothing.

'I am at my wits' end. I am at the end of my tether,' Margaret said.

'The child needs the challenge of a complete change of scene,' Vincent said.

So when Eva and Bedrock and Carrillo went home to Copperfield, they took Virginia with them. At the railway station, Dr O'Day took a photograph of the travellers. He imagined they were Russian exiles standing on Victoria Station thinking about the royal family in Ekaterinburg.

Bedrock Remembers the Journey from Launceston to Copperfield

The first time I saw Virginia was when she was in her father's car and he came to get me and Rosie and Doll from the Gorge. Doll wouldn't go on the suspension bridge, and so Rosie and I waited with her while her father went to get the car. I was grateful to Doll for that because I was too scared to cross the bridge as well, but I was also too scared to say so. Virginia was

very, very thin, and her head seemed to wobble on her neck
like a flower on a stem. I thought she looked like a poppy. She
came back to Copperfield with us. At the station in Launceston
I bought the *Australasian Post* to read on the train and Dr O'Day
made us all line up on the platform while he took a photograph.
For the whole journey Virginia sat in the corner of the carriage
with her brown overcoat buttoned up, completely silent. She
ate nothing and drank nothing and spent most of her time just
staring out the window. Carrillo and I tried to get her to talk,
but she was silent and dreamy and remote. I was afraid of her.
As well as looking like a flower, she resembled a witch.

On the cover of my *Australasian Post* was a woman in a bath-
ing suit, and inside the magazine were stories about strange
and terrible things with smudgy black-and-white photographs
to illustrate them. I kept returning to one story in particular. It
was about a father who kissed his children goodbye one morning and never saw them alive again because the house caught
fire and the children were burnt to death. Next to the story was
a photograph of the burnt bodies of the children in their bed.
Although it was a black-and-white picture, I thought the burnt
children looked like stewed apricots. Like when you take ripe
apricots and split them and put them in a saucepan with water and sugar, and you bring the water to the boil and let the
fruit simmer until it is soft. The round lumps of apricot lie with
puckered and wrinkled skins in the water that is thick with
mush and shiny with sugar.

I kept closing the magazine and folding it up and putting it
on the seat beside me. Then I would be compelled to look at
the picture as if I were looking for clues to something. Then
I would re-read the story. The story did not explain why the
house burnt down. I wondered what had caused the fire, and
where the children's mother was. Because the story offered no
explanations to these questions, it was a deeply frightening story, and very sad. Could a house burn down for no reason with
helpless sleeping children inside? Whose fault was it? Who was

to blame?

Members of my family often told the story of the burning of the old Palace Hotel in Queenstown, and they always gave as the reason for the fire the fact that a woman had been smoking in bed while drinking a bottle of the best brandy in the house. But in the story in the *Post*, the man kissed the children and the children said goodbye Daddy, and when the man came home that night they were dead. Their voices, he said, as they farewelled him in the morning, were unusually sad. He said they seemed to know they were doomed. 'I kissed them and they put their arms around me and they just said goodbye Daddy and then they seemed to look straight into my heart and I went to the door and they waved and said it again and I went out the gate and crossed the railway line and they waved again. Then they must have gone back to bed. It was very early and it was cold. And that was all.'

As I stared over and over at the picture, I wondered who had taken the photograph of the dead children. I wondered where their father was when the photograph was being taken. Why had he let somebody take this picture of the bubbly remains of his children in the twisted black iron skeleton of their bed? Or had the father perhaps taken the photograph himself? Was he, like Dr O'Day, taking photographs at every opportunity? If two of his children lay charred remains in a ruined bed, would Dr O'Day take photographs? I thought he probably would. It seemed odd to me that the *Post* had not put in a picture of those children when they were alive. A smiling picture of a child with wide clear eyes and smooth fat cheeks. I had seen things like that. Pictures of children's bodies in ditches alongside portraits of the same children on Father Christmas's knee.

The photograph and the story in the *Post* still rise unbidden to the surface of my mind. I think of it and I am back in the railway carriage opening and closing the magazine and then folding it up and sitting on it. Then I take it out and open it so that I can look again and again at the picture and read about the children's voices. I look out of the carriage window when the train has stopped at a country station. A man and a child get off the train, and as we continue on our journey they walk across a ploughed paddock. The soil is good for growing potatoes. The man holds the child's hand as they cross the paddock. From time to time the child looks back at the train and I wonder if she can see me looking at her. They are walking towards a farmhouse that is partly obscured by dark pine trees. The man and the child get smaller and smaller; the train goes round a bend, and the man and the child are lost forever.

Carrillo and I could talk to each other about Virginia on the train. We talked in our own language of Meaning, and knew that most of the time Virginia would not know what we were saying, although she knew we were talking about her. Eva tried to stop us from doing this by telling us a story. The story she told us was the one about the snow child whose parents made her from snow and then put her in front of the fire by mistake so that the child melted and was no more. As I remember all this, I see how close my thoughts must have been running with Eva's. Perhaps she also read the story of the father and his children, and saw the man and the child crossing the paddock.

We were sitting opposite Virginia who was so pale and thin and silent she might have been dead or dying. I thought she looked transparent and possessed of some knowledge and wisdom I did not understand. The photograph above her was a picture of thick, dense, graceful, mysterious and menacing ferns. It was a very old photograph that was so faded it was going green. The words underneath the picture meant to say it was a picture of man-ferns at the limestone caves near Mole Creek.

Letters were missing so that the notice read: 'Ma ferns at the liestone caves ear ole reek.' Carrillo and I thought this was very funny and we sniggered so much we got on Eva's nerves.

During that train journey, perhaps as a result of the picture and story in the *Post,* I began to imagine that when we got home the Palace Hotel would not be there. My parents would have moved into the rooms where Eva lived above the Bluebird Café. Or my parents would have perished in the fire at the Palace. I used to be afraid, when I was a child, that my mother and father existed only when I was near them. I had put this idea out of my mind all the time we had been away, but as we got closer to Copperfield, I began to play with thoughts of their disappearance. I knew they could just dissolve when I was not there to protect them and make them real. I imagined going home to find empty spaces where my mother and father had been. They would be blank outlines in the air above the smouldering ashes of the Palace. They would not even be lumps of stewed apricot. I began to prepare for the shock of the sight of the blanks where my parents had been.

Years and years after this, I saw a photograph taken of the children at my daughter's birthday party when she was, I think, six. The photograph I was looking at was already about twenty years old, and it had faded and cracked. But the most striking thing about it was that silverfish had attacked it in such a way that the place where Lovelygod should have been was a blank just like the blank I had imagined when I was on the train going home to Copperfield. Lovelygod is gone from sight, and her image has disappeared from this photograph. Sometimes I imagine that just as the silverfish worked to remove her from the picture, some force unknown to me dissolved her in the reality of her bedroom at the end of the verandah. Three walls of Lovelygod's verandah were made from windows. In one of these walls was a flimsy wooden door that was never locked. The door was painted white, and the window frames were white also. The cupboards were white, with dolls sitting on top of them, and there was a mirror and a small bed with a white counterpane. The curtains on the window were calico with yellow daisies stencilled around the edge. In this sweet white room of glass, in the middle of the quiet night, when all people, dogs and horses were sleeping, a blue light blazed through the windows and fell upon the child who in that moment ceased to be. Her blankets flattened out in the place where she had slept, holding for a time like an envelope the heat her body had left behind.

In the years since Lovelygod disappeared from her bed I have imagined many, many strange ways she could have gone. I have also remembered things from books that I have read, things that seem sometimes to hold hidden clues to the mystery. I remember when Pinocchio ran from his assassins and arrived breathless at the door of the small white house among the dark green trees. In desperation he kicked the door and beat his head against it. A lovely little girl came to the window. She had blue hair and a face as white as wax, but her eyes were closed and her hands were crossed on her breast. Without moving her lips in the least she said in a soft little voice that seemed to come from another world:

'There is no one in this house. They are all dead.'
'Then open the door to me yourself.'
'I am dead, too.'

Everything that seems to be a clue is a red herring. I sometimes say that over to myself: 'Every clue is a red herring.' Then I imagine a perfect red fish, not red like blood, but bright glittering orange, and this fish is made from metal but it is alive somehow. It is tied to a string that is being pulled by a mysterious and invisible person and this invisible one moves at great speed, darting, leaping, rushing through the ice and snow of highland lakes, through the breathing darkness of forests unexplored, down the paved and ringing streets of the towns where people in fashionable overcoats pause for a minute and turn back and stare.

When Lovelygod disappeared, she was the same age as my brother and I were when we went on the train. We were ten. We were all ten then, me and Carrillo and Lovelygod. I remember how full of life we were, how I could feel life bubbling and laughing inside me, springing out from behind my eyes. 'Just look at her bright eyes,' people would say, 'and her fiery topaz curls.' I imagine the three of us at the age of ten, Carrillo and me so big and bright, Lovelygod so small and white and beautiful. We are going to the amusement park I have heard they have built on the hill where Trevallyn used to be. Part of the amusement park is a replica of Copperfield as it was long ago. We visit the replica of the Palace Hotel and the Bluebird Café, and we marvel at statues of ourselves, in the waxworks museum. When I remember how full of life I was, I cannot at all understand how the ten-year-old life of my daughter was stopped, removed, filleted out of the world, leaving only the unruffled envelope of her bed.

In the twenty years since Lovelygod disappeared, I have never given up hope of finding her. Perhaps such hope is the same thing as madness. While everyone in the world save Carrillo and I has stopped searching, we are unable to stop. Carrillo's search is in the world; mine is in my mind and spirit, in my heart. I read over and over the stories of other lost children. Some of these children are the real children of real parents whose stories are written in newspapers and journals and books; some of them are children in literature. I have come to realize that the idea of a lost child is quite a common idea in stories.

From my grandfather's library I brought many books, and much of my time I spend in reading. It is strange to think that the replica of Copperfield is, in its own way, alive, while all of the Copperfield of my childhood has shrunk to the Bluebird Café where I live, and read the books from the library. When I come upon the Lost Child in a book that I am reading, I am for a short time excited and elated as if Lovelygod is coming back to me. The Lost Child of literature in this way consoles and sustains me; the lost children in the newspapers fill me only with dread, and wind me in a tangle of despair.

I keep two kinds of notebook, one is for notes from literature where the Lost Child lives, and the other is for notes from life where the lost children are still missing. Again and again I read the part in *The Hunchback of Notre Dame* where Gudule, the Recluse, living in the Rat Hole, is reunited with her daughter, Agnes, after fifteen years during which Gudule has almost believed the child to have been eaten by the Egyptians who stole her. Gudule shows the girl the little embroidered shoe that belonged to Agnes. From a little bag adorned with green beads which she wears about her neck, the girl removes the matching shoe.

The highlight of the story of *Cinderella* is for me the moment when the prince found the glass slipper fitted Cinderella as if it had been made of wax, and when Cinderella took from her pocket the other slipper and put it on her foot. I have called it the highlight of the story, but I should have said I find that moment of the matching of the shoes to be the *point* of the story. It is the moment when the reader's heart leaps for joy with the sense that the circle has closed. I read *Cinderella* again and again to get to the point where she takes from her pocket the other slipper and puts it on her foot.

In the shop window in Devonport I used to see a pair of shoes identical to the shoes Shirley Thompson was wearing when she disappeared. Nobody has told me, but I know in my heart that Shirley Thompson has never been found. However, I have always imagined the moment when the two pairs of shoes might have been matched. This moment is less heart-leaping than the moment when two shoes of one pair are reunited, matched.

I used to get a lot of information about disappearing children from all over the world. Occasionally people still send me things. I received an item from the *China Mail* of 15 May 1878. As if in the passage of a hundred years the story in the *China Mail* might shed some light on the mystery of my daughter. The story said: 'Young children are bought or stolen at a tender age and placed in a vase with a narrow neck, the vase having a movable base. In this receptacle the unfortunate little wretches are kept for years in a sitting posture, their heads outside being all the while carefully tended and fed. When the child has reached the age of twenty or over, he or she is taken away to some distant place and "discovered" in the woods as a wild man or woman.'

I did not believe a word of this story because the details are filled with impossibilities. Yet it is another small chapter in the story of *The Lost Child*. I look at it and I see that its fantastic suppositions are no more bizarre than one of the ideas that I have allowed to dwell in my heart. This is the idea that Lovelygod was taken by the land itself.

In Lovelygod's blood, something was missing, something that urges children's bodies on until they grow to the size of adults and then stop growing. Lovelygod was like a perfect little doll-child who would never, the doctors said, stand more than three feet high. Her blood was a mixture of streams of blood that came flowing in bright channels from England, Ireland, and the Portland tribe, that came flowing and emptied themselves in this tiny white vessel-child. She was conceived in the passion that used to exist between Carrillo and me. By outside standards she was a freak, and so beautiful.

I imagine the middle of that night when she was lost. I cannot say I remember that middle of the night because I was asleep, and it seemed to me to be a night like any other night. It was cold, but the nights are often cold in Copperfield. So I imagine the night. The land has been robbed of its copper; where the dark giants of trees once stood run little roads and streets and slippery laneways. The water in the streams is poisoned; barren hillsides where no plant will grow shine in the light of the moon. The interior of the forest is dim and moist, for sunlight can not penetrate the thick foliage, and the forest floor lies still and soft and mossy like the bed of a silent giant. Beneath the canopy of the great myrtles are soft festoons of fungi. In the dark grey-green of this forest where the fronds and swords and slow coils of ferns criss and cross and curl like some memory more than half forgotten in the mind, scarlet, spongy caps gleam in rotting crevices, and the silence of the secret glades is the silence of a nightmare. In some places the forest floor is false, a laughing trick of the land, a trap.

I hear the silence of the forest reaching out to Lovelygod and calling her in the middle of the night from her bed. In her white nightgown she runs through the back garden of the Palace, past rows of vegetables and fruit trees, until she comes to the wire gate that opens onto the gravel path leading away, away into the forest. On bare and frozen feet she runs into the thickest darkness of the smoky labyrinth; she goes where none but darting, furry animals may go. In and in and in she skips until she reaches the false floor of the phantom forest, treads on the magic carpet of sweet, poisonous matting, and slips through the surface and is gone. No ruffle, no ripple, no sound can be detected outside the forest. When the child was born, I thought that she had wings. Had she wings they would not save her now for she could flutter forever in the cage the earth has made for her.

In an essay, Graham Greene wrote: 'In childhood all books are books of divination, telling us about the future, and like the fortune teller who sees a long journey in the cards or death by water they influence the future.' Sometimes I take those words in a literal way and I recall how so many of the stories and po-ems I used to read over and over as a child in my grandfather's library dealt in some way with the Lost Child. Then I imagine that those things I read were warning me about what was going to happen, preparing me for the future and the worst. I imagine also that by reading those things I was infected by Lost Child Disease. If I had not read those books, Lovelygod would not have disappeared.

We used to have concerts at the Gaiety Theatre. One time I recited:

> Come away oh human child
> To the waters and the wild

With a faery hand in hand
For the world's more full of weeping
Than you can understand.

Now I wonder whether the poem was warning me or leading me. I try to forget I ever said it; try to pretend it was never written, that W. B. Yeats never existed.

To begin with, after the copper ran out and people left and people died, they would say to me you can't stay here hoping for the rest of your life. If Lovelygod is ever found, you will be told and reunited with her. You don't have to wait here in Copperfield. But I knew I did have to wait here, that if she was coming back from where she had been, or coming back from the dead, she would come here, and I would be waiting. As the big houses emptied and the insects and animals and the forest began to inhabit them, and they began to rust and split and crumble, I stayed in the place I have always loved best, the Bluebird Café, where I keep a long and holy vigil, warmed by the wood that burns in the stove. I have kerosene lanterns and tanks for the water.

I am slowly returning to a primitive existence, although I have not yet reached the simplicity of the life of my grandparents when they were making their way along the Welcome River towards Copperfield after the hotel had been burnt down in Queenstown. I think of their journey. Sometimes they found a cave or an abandoned hut in which to shelter. The huts which used to be found in this area were built by the South-West people to be used during their seasonal migrations. They used to dig out the earth and then build a hut over the depression. The hut was dome-shaped, with one small, low doorway. The roof was thatched with long grass and lined with tea-tree bark, decorated with the feathers of wild birds.

My grandfather used to tell me that inside one of these huts he found a drawing of the moon in charcoal. Sometimes they came to cleared areas where the South-West people had burnt out the vegetation. At such times, my grandmother used to say, she felt as if the land were inviting them to sit down, rest, and have a meal. In her diary my grandmother wrote: 'The forest was thick and dark and inhospitable. One day when the rain had stopped we came to a clearing. The grass was covered with fragile blue flowers on long, thin stalks, and because the stalks were almost invisible, the flowers formed a mist above the grass. We sat down among the flowers in the rare and golden sunshine and partook of a breakfast of thick plum pudding and scalding tea with sugar. When we continued on our way, the wet and rotting vegetation underfoot seemed to have become more treacherous for our having stopped to rest.' I think of the hardships of my grandparents' lives, and see myself living here in strange, still comfort.

The little railway in from the coast has not run for many years. Sometimes I have walked along the railway line, using the overgrown track as a pathway. A disused railway line is a haunted thing. Cut like a wound through the rocks, between the giant trees, the old line still snakes along from Copperfield to the sea. The road in from the coast was never sealed, and is by now a wreck, yet people still brave it and come to see the ghost town. People come to talk to me. In a way, I must be the ghost.

Before Lovelygod was born, when Carrillo and I were in America, we went to Colorado, and in Colorado there was a ghost town called Leadville. We had never seen a ghost town, and so we went to Leadville to have a look. It was not as empty as Copperfield is. There were a few shops and people. But once it had been a thrilling, sparkling town because of the silver mines. We saw the remains of mansions and the opera house and I never imagined then that what I was seeing was a fore-shadowing of what would happen in Copperfield. There was a house with a picture of a huge eye painted under the gable which curved over like an eyelid.

In a book I bought in the dingy paper shop there, I read

about the ice palace. One winter in Leadville they built a vast pleasure palace of ice. All winter long they skated and gambled and danced in the ice palace, and in the spring, the palace melted and they never built one again. I read in the book about the life of Baby Doe Tabor, who was the wife of a rich silver king. The Tabors lived like royalty in Leadville until they lost their fortune in the silver panic in 1893. One of their daughters was named Rose Mary Echo Silver Dollar Tabor, known as Honeymaid. When we named Lovelygod we were influenced, I think, by all the names of Honeymaid Tabor. Another name I read in a book and liked, a long time ago, was Lavender Christmas Ashby. And once I heard of a girl called Catherine Fairy Peacock. I have thought of writing a book that begins, 'Lovelygod Mean was born with wings.' Then I would tell the story of my daughter's life, and when she was ten she would take flight. But then the ending of the story would be just a fairy-tale that says, 'She spread her wings and soared up, up into the night sky and she flew on and on in the solitude of the mountain darkness until she was a speck, and then she was lost from sight. Lovelygod was never seen again.' The reader of the fairy-tale takes this ending on faith, and turns the page to begin the next story.

I can never end the story like that. Lovelygod has not disappeared completely; Lovelygod is coming back.

When I read the book about Leadville, I was saddened by the story of the last years of Baby Doe's life. She lived alone in a primitive cabin on the site of her own Matchless mine which she always hoped to re-open. She died there, penniless but always hopeful, in 1935, and was found there frozen stiff in the form of a cross. The book contained a photograph of the inside of Baby Doe's cabin after it had been ransacked by people who were searching for hidden treasure. The most horrible part about this to me was that Baby Doe was lying there dead when the looters were tearing the sparse furniture apart. They found nothing of value, and they left the body where they had found it. A thing I thought very sad was the way Baby Doe, in the last

years of her life, when she lived alone in the cabin with her ob-
session, wore boots made by wrapping pieces of burlap round
her feet, and tying the whole thing up with twine. Ever since I
read about that, and saw the photographs of Baby Doe with her
burlap boots, so long ago, I have thought how pleased I am to
have real leather boots.

My thoughts have travelled far from my memories of the
train journey we took from Launceston to Copperfield when
we were children. On that journey I was carrying with me a gift
for my parents and a souvenir for myself. The gift was a large
paper bag full of the bright pink lollies they used to make at
a shop in Launceston. They were called jockey caps because
that's what they looked like, and they were made from thin toffee filled with coconut ice. The souvenir was a piece, about half
a yard, of pretty material I bought in a draper's shop. It was a
piece of white cotton printed with designs of blue peacocks and
pink blossom trees, and it was the first piece in my collection of
cloth. I have been collecting ever since. In the last few years I
have begun to sort these pieces, and to cut them up and arrange
them in patchwork designs. Sometimes I sew the patchwork
by hand, and sometimes I use the sewing machine that used to
belong to my mother.

Someone from The Best People came and tried to buy the
machine from me so they could put it in the replica they have
made of the Palace Hotel. Most things went, but I would not
part with the sewing machine. When I have finished making
one of my quilts, Jack Fisher, who brings in my supplies from
Woodpecker Point, takes the quilt back with him and somebody sells it. Once when I put some pieces of the peacock and
blossom material in a quilt, the woman who bought the quilt
came all the way from Hobart to ask me about those pieces of
cloth. I told her I had bought the fabric when I was a child, and
she told me that when she was a child living on a sheep station
in New South Wales she had nursery curtains made from my
material. That was why she came to see me. Then years later, a

parcel came from her. She had been back to the sheep station and had got the nursery curtains which she then sent to me. I still have those curtains hanging in one of the rooms upstairs. Such acts of kindness and goodness and coincidence as what that woman did, nourish me with hope. The hope that is always being nourished in this way is the hope that Lovelygod will come back. My mind returns always to this point.

Occasionally when he brings the supplies, Jack brings me a newspaper, but not very often. What I like doing is taking scraps of newspaper wrapping from some of the things he brings and reading what is on them. I read half of one story and half of another depending on the way the paper is torn. I learned from one of the scraps that there is a place at Cape Grim now called an atmospheric-control centre. Twice I have got a page from a mainland newspaper where they advertise things to do that remind me of the things you could do in California thirty years ago. You can learn foot reflexology or the principles of social-role valorization and its application to human services. There are lifestyle seminars in motherhood burnout and polarity therapy courses in transforming confusion into wisdom.

We are referred to in mainland newspapers as 'the Tasmanians'. When I see this written I think it has a very historic air. As if we are actually a particular race. I read that 'the Tasmanians have opened a hang-gliding simulator over the edge of an 18 metre cliff on the outskirts of Launceston'. Jack had to explain that to me the next time he came. People ride on a cable, imitating people who imitate birds. Because I talk to so few people, and do not listen to the radio, and read only scattered snatches from the newspapers, I sense that the English language has gone beyond a point where I can understand it.

I understand neither the people nor their language nor their lives. Carrillo is out there in the world learning the language and the ways as he searches for Lovelygod. He wrote to me from Italy a year ago, but that is the last I have heard. Perhaps he is getting closer to where she is. I wonder whether I will be able to understand his language when he comes back. It is possible that Lovelygod does not speak English very much at all. Perhaps she has never heard it spoken since she was ten. Carrillo and I will always have Meaning even if our English is different. I have heard that in New Guinea there are 450 different languages because groups of people have been isolated from each other by the mountains and rivers. Carrillo and I are the only people in the world who speak Meaning, and I could become the only person who speaks Bedrock English.

BOOK TWO ·
COPPERFIELD

In childhood all books are books of
divination, telling us about the future,
and like the fortune teller who sees a long
journey in the cards or death by water
they influence the future.

Graham Greene, *The Lost Childhood*

Copperfield 1950

It was a day at the end of winter that Eva Mean brought Bedrock and Carrillo and Virginia O'Day back to Copperfield. On the night of Friday 1 September, Virginia began to write in her diary.

> I am sad and lonely and I am very far from home. Today I have eaten nothing. I came here to Copperfield with Eva Mean and her niece and nephew to stay with my uncle and aunt. I was able to get away from home without touching my breakfast, although I pretended I had nibbled on the Weetbix. I broke some off and crumbled it up in my pocket. Here with my aunt and cousins it will be different, and I will have to work out some different tricks. I drank some water when the train stopped at Devonport. I escaped to

my room tonight without any dinner; I said I was too tired out by travelling. Tomorrow I must look for some scales in the bathroom. At home my mother hid them and so I had to weigh myself in town. The last time I checked I was six and a half stone. I am working to lose the extra half stone. The last time I wrote to you, Dear Diary, I told you I was just under eight stone. That was last Christmas and since then I have been too miserable and unhappy to face you and reveal to you my thoughts. Now that I am in Copperfield, I have gone beyond that unhappiness to a deep loneliness in which I find I must once again confide in you or I will go mad.

My pen has not been idle since I last wrote to you. I have done the outlines of about three novels, and I have also kept up my notebooks and lists. With the novels, I don't know why I can't get past the first chapters. The outlines go really well, but then I do the first chapter, and I get excited about that, but I can't make the second chapter come to life. It is not that I lose interest; I seem to lose some necessary kind of energy. I know I have you to talk to, but I must confess I long to be able to talk to someone who has already written books. I have wondered whether I should stop doing such detailed outlines. It's as if I feel I have written the whole thing when all I have done is the outline. I am never lost for ideas for the outlines.

I have decided that writing to you will help me to overcome this problem, and I have decided to try very hard to finish the whole novel of *Savage Paradise*. I began it in the cemetery. I got so carried away with the writing that I was late getting home and my father caught me and then they decided to send me up here for some fresh air and exercise and things like that. They also think I won't be able to resist the eggs and cream and potatoes. They don't understand the first thing about me, of course.

Savage Paradise is a love story, really an historical romance, about a Scottish girl who comes to Van Diemen's Land and falls in love and marries and has to cope with all the problems of the convict servants and the bushrangers and the blacks. Before she comes here she imagines it will be like Scotland, but with butterflies and tropical flowers and dear little furry animals and colourful birds. When she gets off the boat in Hobart she is dismayed to find that many of the people still live in wattle and daub huts, and lead harsh and miserable lives. However, her parents receive a grant of land in the north of the island, at White Hills, and they gradually become prosperous farmers with a fine country house. She falls in love with the young man who is the son of the people on a nearby property. Although the land is not the paradise she expected, she comes to see that it is a wild, dark version of a kind of paradise she could never have imagined.

Something I am going to miss about Launceston is the public library. I need to be able to look up reference books for many of the details in the novel. I have heard that there is some sort of a library here belonging to the Means, but I don't imagine it would be much good for what I want. However, I will ask if it is possible for me to see it just in case it has anything useful. Perhaps there will be an encyclopaedia. For that matter, I suppose my cousins will own an encyclopaedia.

I should tell you about the awful thing that happened the other night at home. I was lying in bed watching the moon through the lace curtains and banging on the wall from time to time to stop Rosie and Bedrock from making so much noise, when I suddenly got this terrible pain in my left ear. I screamed

out and they got my father to come and see what had
happened. Daddy looked in my ear and then he said
he thought some kind of insect had got in. He said he
thought it might be a cockroach. I stopped screaming
because I nearly fainted from shock and disgust. I have
never ever imagined a cockroach crawling into my ear.
I have thought about earwigs, and sometimes I have
brushed my hand across the pillow before putting my
head down on it just in case there was an earwig there.
And once, as you know, Dear Diary, I used to check
the pillow very carefully in case Rosie had put needles
in it. The pain of the cockroach was unbelievable, and
in the end I did faint. Daddy got the cockroach out in
sections and put drops in my ear. Then he gave me an
injection of penicillin and he sent around to Mr Quinlan in the morning for some penicillin chewing gum
which I hate. I wonder how many calories it has got.

The cockroach stands for everything I hate about
home. The house is so untidy and so dirty, and I think
nobody but me seems to notice or care. Belinda is
meant to be there to help keep it clean and tidy, but
she is so busy ironing frilly bonnets for Doll and wip-
ing Doll's nose that she hardly ever gets out a duster.
My mother is so fat. She is fat and disgusting and she
is so busy doing good works in the world and working
for charity she wouldn't even know if I fell down dead.
I can tell all this to you alone, my secret heart. Imagine, if you will, being a girl who sleeps in a bedroom
where cockroaches are so numerous and so fearless
they will crawl into the ear of a sleeping girl.

The cockroach crawls, scurries, from behind the
ancient skirting board. Dangling above it, it can see
the fringe of the bedspread. It hooks on to this fringe
with its feathery black claws and moves up, up until
it comes to the frilly cuff of the nightgown. The cock-

roach darts and dances up the flowered sleeve and shivers with rapture when it discovers a trailing lock of hair. It swings on to the silken curl and slithers along until it reaches the place where the ear lies open. The ear is a maze of gutters, pink-warm-and-perfect, leading into a deep, mysterious, sweet darkness. Before long the creature is trapped in the soft pocket in the girl's head, and as it struggles to escape, it causes the girl to scream with pain. The cockroach is looking for an arrow, for a sign marked EXIT, for a trail of stones, for a silken thread. It turns in the little space it has, and as it turns, the girl imagines that a wheel composed of steel needles is turning in her head. At the thought of this, she faints.

Afterwards I thought about how the cockroach might have burrowed into my brain. It could have eaten away the part that is good at mathematics and Latin. Or it could have chewed up the section that writes novels. Or it might have caused my body to start manufacturing layers and layers of fat. It could easily have caused deafness, quite easily. If I was deaf as well as fat and ugly, I would certainly kill myself. I live in fear of suffering from disabilities. What if a bee came and stung you in the eye on the actual eyeball. I mention bees because Uncle Brendan has bees and I am frightened of them. My aunt has been sending us pots of honey for years. It is delicious honey. However, I had never thought about what it is like to have bees in the garden.

The bees here are in a long box that stands on the stumps of two old plum trees. The box has small round windows with glass in them, and is divided into many compartments like drawers. As one compartment is filled with honey, the bees leave it and go to another compartment. Then my uncle comes along and takes the honey from the filled section. This way you can get the honey without disturbing the bees. When you look through the windows which are just like portholes, you can see the bees at work, and they look horrible. As they seethe about the hive they give the impression they are still and yet moving at the same time. It is impossible to follow the activity and progress of any one bee because they all move all the time. They are so fat and hairy and self-sufficient and busy and noisy.

I felt very strange when I was standing at the hive looking in at the bees through the glass. They were crawling and pushing and stirring, and I felt very big, the way you do when you are standing in front of a dolls' house. And yet this was different because I felt that the bees were more powerful than I was. They seemed to have a secret; and I knew they could kill me if they attacked me.

I once heard of a man who died from just one bee sting. I have never been stung, but last summer Doll was stung twice. I had taken her to the park by the river. I couldn't make her wear her shoes, and she ran in bare feet through the clover beside the swing. She was stung on the heel. I said she would have to put her shoes on or she would get stung again, but she refused to put them on. She went running across the clover to the rocks by the water and a bee got her on the other foot. Both her feet swelled up fast after the second sting and she couldn't walk and she cried and cried. I had to carry her all the way home and then I was in trouble for not looking after her properly. The silly little thing still doesn't wear shoes and I think she must be retarded.

The mention of retarded brings me to a point about Copperfield. I am secretly afraid of the freaks here.

This place is one of the remotest towns in Tasmania, and I know that in these places there are not just people who are idiots, but there are people who have the face of a pig or a dog. They have people who are half human or half wolf in these places. There is a brand of butter that comes from Duck River and nobody will eat it at home because it is made by people with feet and hands like ducks. I have to confess I have seen no evidence of this sort of thing here yet, but on the way in from the coast we came through a terrible forest called the Back Woods, and I could see and feel that it was just the sort of place where those people would live. The trees were tall and dark and close together and you couldn't see any houses or even smoke, but I could feel the presence of eyes watching us.

There is something definitely strange about Bedrock and Carrillo Mean. They are identical except for the fact that one is a girl and the other a boy. I have never seen twins like them. They are like two parts of one person, or more like two manifestations of one being. Their hair has an unearthly beauty resembling the hair of angels in some paintings. They talk to each other in a secret language and are consequently ill-mannered and sly. On the train Bedrock kept opening and closing a very unpleasant-looking magazine. She would fold it up and sit on it, and then she would take it out again and start opening it and closing it and folding it and twisting it round and round. She was very irritating to be near. I stayed half-turned away from her, but I could still see her fidgetting out of the corner of my eye. I was looking out the window most of the time, and the scenery, especially when we were going along the coast after we left Burnie, was beautiful. The sand is white. I pretended I was on a train in the south of France.

I have told you before, many times, Dear Diary, of how I long to get away from here, to escape. I want to escape from my family and from the people I know, who are, generally speaking, very dull. I think of this island as a cul-de-sac, a trap, into which a handful of poor little insects have fallen. A few of these insects are able to crawl feebly out and fly to distant bright beautiful places, but most of them huddle and worry around in the damp and dark of the trap, going blind and deaf and ending up dead in the bottom of the bag with all the remains of the insects that have gone before them. Glittering scales and glowing transparent wings gather in jagged mounds.

At present I am in the weirdest and most remote part of the island. I like it better here than in the stifling little towns. I am far, far out on the edge of nowhere. My father wants me to train to be a schoolteacher in Hobart. I am supposed to get married then and settle down in Tasmania forever. 'Settle down' suggests to me that I am now an active volcano, but if I do the right things I will stop exploding and bubbling and seething and throwing up rocks, and I will gradually become less and less active and will eventually settle down and then go to sleep and then die altogether.

I thought one way of getting out might be to join a religious order, but I haven't got a vocation. Worse than that, since I last wrote to you, I have lost my faith. I am now dedicated only to fasting and literature. I read and I write and I do not eat. I will continue to lose weight and I will continue to write *Savage Paradise*, and when the book is published I will be so thin, and there will be so many shocking scenes of violence and passion in the novel that I will be forced to leave home in disgrace. Nobody here will want to know me. I will have said terrible things about Tasmania and

I will go to stay with one of my mother's cousins in France which is all I will be fit for. I will say the native women and the convict women were raped; I will say the Aborigines were murdered. Then, as thin as anybody can possibly be, I will go to live in France. I will take with me some of my books such as Jane Austen, Virginia Woolf and Emily Brontë. I will also take my snow domes. My mother would not let me bring them to Copperfield, my domes, that is. She said there would be plenty for me to do here without having to mope in the corner staring into little glass balls. I miss my miniature worlds, and I can't see that there is much to do here. However, I will be able to write, and that is the main thing.

I will write in my aunt's garden which is very pretty, like something in a story-book. Everyone says it is a miracle she can get so many things to grow because of the mine, but she says she will not let a thing like a copper mine defeat her. She is determined to have a garden that resembles her grandmother's garden in Surrey.

My aunt's house is also pretty, and it is spotless. This fact was a great relief to me because I was afraid the house would be dreadful, even made from hessian bags and mud with only the earth for a floor. On the contrary, it is a grand brick and sandstone house with graceful verandahs and elegant designs in the coloured glass of the windows. My uncle said they got the windows from Melbourne and they nearly lost them because the ship they were on was practically wrecked in a storm in Bass Strait.

The Palace Hotel is also very grand. I had heard about it, but I never imagined it would be as lovely as it is. I plan to go and see what it is like inside, and I will go to the Bluebird Café where, I am told, there

are photographs of my family on the wall. The trouble
with the Bluebird Café is that I will be expected to eat
things if I go there. People are forever talking about
Eva Mean's cooking. It is certainly strange for me to
be planning to go out like this because for months I
have stayed in my bedroom in Trevallyn except when
I went out for secret walks to the cemetery or the library or the museum.

There might be a problem about going to mass on
Sunday. I have decided that the only thing to do is to
tell my aunt I have abandoned my faith, as there is no
use pretending. When I was a child I had a naive faith,
but this was shattered by the senseless and inexplica-
ble deaths of Brenda Lacey and Father Moloney. Brenda was not a special friend of mine, but I used to go to
her birthday parties when we were younger, and she
was in my class at school. She had a summer house
at the bottom of the garden where we always had the
party. Brenda was sweet and kind and very pretty with
long, blonde curls, and her mother was good at making butterfly cakes. They had a creek that ran through
the garden, and willow trees and a little boat. Then,
just after her fifteenth birthday, Brenda started having
headaches and seeing double and losing weight, and
eventually they found out about the tumour. It was on
her brain, and by the time they found out what it was,
it was much too late to have an operation and Brenda
just sank into this blank, mad pain. I believe that in
the end she died of starvation because there was no
longer any point feeding her through the vein and so
they stopped doing it.

Before she died we had novenas all the time for
her and everybody prayed for a miracle. Her mother and father gave her a horse called Strawberry for
her fifteenth birthday but I think she only ever rode

him about three times. I can't understand why Brenda was made to suffer like that and die. But in fact, what I can't understand is why she ever lived. Fifteen years of being good and sweet and kind and pretty and having parties and a boat and a horse and then ... eternal life or eternal death. Everlasting light or perpetual darkness. Because I can no longer believe in eternal life, I must believe in eternal death and nothingness.

The same week that Brenda died, Father Moloney got up on the table in the presbytery dining room to change a light globe and he was electrocuted. He had said the mass for Brenda and after his dinner he was electrocuted there and then, before the housekeeper even had time to take away the remains of the summer pudding and the jug of water with half a lemon in it. I know about those things because Belinda told my mother. Belinda went over to the presbytery to take back the washing, and although she didn't see the body, she saw the table where Father Moloney fell, and the knife and spoon still on the floor.

I was overwhelmed by the meaninglessness of those two deaths, and I abandoned any belief I had had in God. When I had done that I began to see that everything was meaningless. Belinda said I was suffering from melancholia and needed exercise and a holiday by the sea. She said her aunt went like me at the same age and was sent to Swansea where she played tennis and billiards and worked with the fishermen catching crayfish in pots. She ended up marrying a man who had a factory where they froze fish and vegetables. I said I couldn't see what any of this had to do with melancholia and my mother said not to be rude.

I used to think there was a purpose in my father's work, but at this time in my life I realized that even what my father does is without any meaning. Day after day my father beams at the patients and tells them to say 'ah' and then he tells them he will have to take out their tonsils and drain their sinuses. He removes their adenoids and he cures their earaches and sends people to get hearing aids. Patients come to the rooms in an endless stream with their sore throats and runny noses and swollen glands. As soon as one is better, another one is ill, and so it goes on. Babies have cleft palates and hare lips and they have to be mended. Then Brenda just dies for no reason and Father Moloney is the fatal victim of a freakish accident. They dam the rivers and make the electricity and send a little bit of it to the presbytery and Father Moloney in the middle of the dinner, stands on the table and holds up his hand to touch the light, and the power of the electricity that has been captured from God's stream enters his fingertips and throws his whole body down across the table and onto the floor and he is alive no longer.

I think of Father Moloney when I brush my hair. I brush and brush and then the hair stands up on end because of the electricity you get from brushing. I imagine Father Moloney with his hair standing on end like mine. His arms fly out and his fingers are splayed as lightning dashes through his body exploding his heart and forcing fountains of blood to spurt from his staring eyeballs. They said that when he fell from the table he broke his neck. It is all so sad and difficult and pointless.

My father was a doctor in New Guinea during the war. I used to think this was heroic and wonderful, but now I simply can't make any sense out of it. The endless curing of the interminable sick. When Daddy came back from the war we went to the mainland to meet him and I remember he seemed very tall but thin and brown. I thought he was not my father. We went to a park where there was a miniature English village surrounded by a hedge. I thought, this man is not my father, as I held his hand and looked down at the little imitation houses with painted-on windows. The houses were not hollow like real houses, or even dolls' houses; they were solid blocks of something with thatch on top. I think the thatch was real. The worst thing was the windows because they were blind and dumb. I remember all this so clearly because as I stood looking I was thinking that the houses were fakes, and my father was fake, and I half realized that I was only an imitation, a copy of something, too.

Afterwards when we were on the boat coming home, I heard my mother telling some other people how much I had enjoyed visiting the miniature village. She told them about my snow domes as if they proved my interest in the village. My mother has never understood that my snow domes are my own secret worlds that are so beautiful because they are placed under glass. I think the most disturbing thing about the village was the way it was open to the sky and to the eyes of all the people who stand by the hedge looking in. The village was very sad and vulnerable. I didn't like it because it was fake, but I still felt sorry for it.

I have wandered from the point of Brenda and Father Moloney. When they both died I suddenly knew very clearly and for certain that what happened to them could easily happen to me. I used to think that I was safe, that I was a special kind of person in an envelope, a membrane, which would keep me safe from polio and tumours and TB and car accidents and murder and drowning. Then Brenda died and it was as if my envelope split like the cocoon of a moth and I was standing there in the sun, naked and waiting to be

shot by a perfect stranger who smiles at me and pulls
the trigger and I cannot scream. I have been shot in
a place near the heart and I fall against a crumbling
stone wall to the sound of terrible laughter. I knew
then not only that I was certain to die, but that I could
die at any old time and it didn't matter at all. My envelope had gone; I was not at all special.

When I was a lot younger, and still safe in my
membrane envelope, I saw a boy killed by a tram. I
was on the tram and a boy of my own age came running alongside the moving tram and tried to jump on.
He slipped and then he slid under the tram and his
legs were caught in the wheels and were cut off. He
died from loss of blood on the grass at the side of the
road and a man put his jacket over him. I had no fear
at that time that I would ever be run over by a tram. I
thought I would never be bitten by a snake; I would
never be in a car crash; I would never be struck by a
mysterious illness. But when Brenda died and Father
Moloney died, and I saw quite plainly that there is no
God, and that everything is just random, I was overcome by the most dreadful fears and I knew there was
no safety anywhere.

I am writing very frankly to you now, Dear Diary,
and you will realize that the pretty stories I used to
tell you about my life were falsehoods and wishful
thinking. I believed in them when I wrote them. You
would never have guessed from what I wrote last year
that my mother was so disgustingly fat, and that my
father is such a boring, grinning fool. You would have
thought I approved of my mother's good works and
all her efforts for charity. I wish my mother loved me
half as much as she loves the orphans from the Girls'
Home.

I have nothing against the orphans personally, but I am very sad and even jealous about the way my parents seem to love those girls so much. Every Sunday three sisters called Violet, Poppy and Lily Heather come to our place and we have to entertain them. They are actually quite sweet and very polite, but I would rather be doing other things. Of course since I stopped eating and retired to my bedroom like a hermit, I have not seen the Heathers. Their hair is cut short like boys' hair and they have the backs of their necks shaved. The Heathers are very polite and they wear green linen dresses that are too long for them, and brown shoes and fawn stockings with darns in them. Their mother is dead and their father has an orchard and he works very long hours with nobody to help him, so that he can't look after the girls. They have tea with us and their father sends us boxes of apples and sometimes a fish. We know them because their mother died of goitre when my father was treating her. Lily told me her mother also had a form of plague, and that her mother haunts the girls in the orphanage.

Every Sunday when my father drives the girls back to the home, the lady at the home says how wonderful it is that he treats the girls like his own children. The lady doesn't know much about how he treats his own children. If you just think of Doll with the runniest nose in the world, and then realize that my father spends his time treating other people's runny noses, you will realize how much attention he pays to us.

Whenever I start thinking about my father like this, I remember the cellar underneath our house.

For about three years my father spent every spare minute he had digging out the cellar. When he had finished there was a huge hole eight feet deep in some

places, and with an area the same as the area of the
house. Then he made rooms in the cellar and one of
the rooms is his dark-room. In the other rooms he
stores things. Apart from books and old furniture and
tools and broken things, the most important objects in
the cellar are my father's photos and negatives.

I imagine a time when the hole in the rock that is
our cellar is all jammed up with photographic negatives side by side by side like crystals in a huge block
of mica. Along comes a herd of elephants and knocks
the house down flat so that number seventeen Trevallyn Avenue, Trevallyn, becomes a jumble of slates and
bricks and stones and splinters of timber and glass.
Even the chimneys topple and the tallest thing standing is the kitchen stove on which is placed a large,
black pot into which has fallen the shattered picture
of Our Lady of Perpetual Succour.

Swiftly the forest grows across the ruins of the
house like scar tissue on a wound, sealing off the cellar with its negatives intact. A million years pass, and
the negatives stick together to form one cellar-shaped,
cellar-sized block. All the images of our lives and
scenery, our bodies and faces and clothes and furniture and toys and pets and food become fused and
confused in a rock of negative, one complex, shining,
solid chunk of archaeology more mysterious than the
Pyramids, stranger than the great rocks at Stonehenge.

When the negative rock is discovered some time in
eternity, the images will be revealed by a special process, and we will have become a new kind of fossil.
The picture of me in my uniform on the first day of
school will be one of the dinosaurs of the future, and
people will come to a great museum to see me with
my felt hat and my gloves and my school case with V.
O'D. in white letters on the side. I will be projected

onto a huge screen and a voice will tell them I am a
Vod from the twentieth century. (My cousin, Geraldine, wasn't allowed to have her initials—G.O'D.—on
her case and so she just had Geraldine.)

They will project the picture of me with the Grade
Two teacher, Miss World, the time she was adjusting
my halo for the Christmas pageant. You would never
guess to look at this charming picture of Miss World
that Miss World had some peculiar habits. She used
to give out the pastels and the pastel books and tell
us to draw pictures of the vase of flowers on the table, and then she would sit on the table next to the
flowers and take off her shoes. She would then pull
up her skirt and undo her suspenders and carefully
roll down her stockings. She folded the stockings up
together and put them on the table next to the vase of
flowers. After that, she painted her toenails with nail
polish. She wiggled her toes while she waited for the
nail polish to dry, and then she unfolded the stockings
and rolled them back up her legs. When she had done
up her suspenders she put on her shoes and told us to
stop drawing and put our books away.

So Miss World will be in the negative rock along
with nearly everybody except my father. I can't think
of a time when he was not holding the camera so that
the creator of all the leaves of negatives will exist only
as the creator, not as an image. The power of his fin-
ger and the angle of his vision will be present but not
his face and hands. Although perhaps some negatives
do exist in the cellar of Vincent and Margaret on their
wedding day. Margaret is so slender and beautiful in
her wedding dress. I am not in the photo because I did
not exist. And yet in a way I did exist because I must
have been conceived only a few hours after the photo
was taken. I was invisibly present in the wedding pho-

to in two un-united portions. Consequently I am there as a type of ghost that is waiting for a signal in order to materialize. My mother is very thin and pretty in this picture, and I have looked at the print of the picture that we have at home, and I have wondered about how such a pretty little person could become so fat and ugly. What did life and time do to her? Were all the fat women with shopping bags and tribes of children once graceful brides with shining hair and shining eyes like Margaret? Yes, all the fat women were once lovely little brides who carried bouquets of lilies.

The lilies have withered and died, and the silk gowns have yellowed and moulded and crumbled, while the dainty hands have mixed and moulded and manufactured jellies and puddings and chocolate cakes with fluffy cream and strawberries and hundreds and thousands, and hundreds and hundreds of legs of roast two-tooth. They have laundered the white linen cloth; they have cleaned the heavy silver, polished the perfect brass; they have mixed sauces and glazes, and plucked from the garden bunches of herbs and armsful of perfumed flowers. They have put the flowers into water in elegant vases and they have placed the vases on tables and surrounded the vases with vessels of pepper and salt and mustard and all manner of sweet and sour condiments, sugar and spice. Snips and snails and puppydogs' tails. (I may be writing a poetry book or a recipe book.) They bake yellow sponge cakes called Lemon Snowdrift, and cream the butter and sugar thoroughly, stirring in the dry ingredients and blending smooth; for the Nectarine Soufflé they beat and beat the whites of eggs until a stiff froth is formed and then they fold and fold the frothy froths into the mixture, lightly. They make creamy ice-cream in three flavours and they pluck fresh fruit from the fruit trees, crisp vegetables from the crisp vegetable garden where rows and rows of beans and peas twine and vine and pop with green, bright juice, and cabbages as blue as moths bunch out and frill and offer welcome shade to sweet pink babies who come there to sleep. The dainty fingers chop the crispy crunchy lettuces with chop chop chop and all is little pieces, strands of lettuce known as mermaid's hair and the locks of hair go green and near transparent onto the prongs of forks. Knives spread with butter things that are spread with butter such as bread and scones and also fruitcake and Christmas pudding sliced into cold slices with boiled threepences inside. Then they start pushing and poking and popping, tossing and slipping and jamming these fruits of the earth, these works of human hands, into their open mouths. The jaws begin to work and the good white teeth, the vigorous pink tongues grind and roll and the saliva begins to flow and bubble as the stomachs drip with smart digestive rivulets and the voices cry for more, more, more. More mushrooms; better Angel Food; jollier jellied bananas; many mounds of Mother's Mandarine and Marshmallow Salad before we die, before we die in an ecstasy of eating in a morris dance of marzipan coated in thick chocolate as dark as sin and dark as crime and dark as whispers in the ears of wandering wizards.

The Romans used to put live mullet into empty glass goblets and watch them die, blood rushing to the surface of the fish's skin. Then the watchers became the diners, and the fish became the meal. Imagine that. Fish out of water.

I am afraid that in time I may be as fat as my mother. I may be able to avoid this if I can continue to have as little as possible to do with food. But, as I have already observed, this is not going to be easy in Copperfield. Although I was mildly pleased to come here because it is a diversion from the suffocating boredom of home, I am worried that my aunt will try to insist I should eat. I might find some inspiration here, but I don't suppose anything very exciting ever happens. However, I must confess, Dear Diary, that I feel optimistic. I am lonely and sad and worried about food, and yet I sense a different feeling here. Perhaps it is as simple as the change of air and scenery, and the freedom from the suffocation of home.

I became aware of this different feeling just after I had been frightened by the bees in the garden. I was standing out there near the beehive, remembering something I read recently about bees, and I started to realize I felt different from the way I felt at home. I was thinking about how no other form of animal life, as far as is known, can produce young without the union of male and female, except bees. This is because queen bees lay fertilized and unfertilized eggs. Depending on the food given to the fertilized eggs, the eggs turn into worker bees which are all females, or else they turn into queens. But the unfertilized eggs produce the drones which are the male bees that will mate with the queens.

The thing I really can't stand about bees is the noise. It is the kind of noise that gets right inside my head so that my whole brain seems to be invaded and taken over by bees, and no brain remains, only the roaring and seething of the bees. Bees are supposed to be messengers between this world and the world of spirits. Imagine if this were true and you could give a bee a message for your great-great-grandmother in the next world; and then you could follow the bee until it came to the entrance to the world of spirits.

Then you would know where the cross-over line was, the border between here and there, the swirling lilac membrane that hangs between reality and everything else. When I first heard of this ability the bees have to move between this world and the other, I imagined that the membrane would be concealed by wild raspberry canes. I probably thought that because raspberries remind me of little red beehives, and because I think the smell of raspberries is the most heavenly smell in the world.

My aunt has given me a blue velvet dressing gown. She said she was surprised I didn't have a dressing gown and then she told me she always plants her sweet peas on the feast of Saint Patrick.

Goodnight, Dear Diary. Today was the first day of spring.

PS. I have just woken up in the night after having a dream. I dreamt I was in the museum at home, and I was searching for the Egyptian mummy. I walked for miles down long and dreadful corridors, past old dark paintings of early settlers and of Aborigines with russet hair like floor mops dipped in ochre. I went past glass cases containing the sad, stuffed bodies of kangaroos with big glass eyes, and moth holes in their fur. There were giant crabs and pterodactyls hanging from the ceiling, and the bones of dinosaurs mixed up with a collection of very beautiful clocks. There were rows of lovely antique chairs, some of them with tapestry seats embroidered by my aunt; and on little tables were emu eggs mounted on elaborate silver stands. I would go up to the guards who sat on stools in the doorways to the rooms, and I would say, Could you please direct me to the Egyptian mummy? But they could not understand what I was saying. I tried to say it in Latin and they only laughed. Then, stand-

ing by a glass case where there was a display of spit-
toons, I saw our dentist, Dr Cherry. He knew what I
was saying, and he smiled and cupped his hands and
held them out to me and said, Spit here, Virginia.
Then he took me by the hand and led me to the dark-
est corner of a small room which was empty save for
the mummy case. The case was covered with designs
of Egyptian gods and writhing snakes, all in much
brighter colours than any colours I have ever seen. Dr
Cherry knocked on the case with his knuckles, making a hollow sound. Then he opened the case which
was empty and he smiled in a quiet and very horrible
way. I became aware that I was all bound up in ancient
brown bandages.

That was all.

I am so pleased you are here, Dear Diary. I got
up and went over to the window and I looked down
into the garden where the beehive was glowing in the
moonlight.

Virginia's Aunt Writes to Virginia's Mother

'Woodlawn'
Copperfield
Saturday, 2 September

My Dear Margaret,

*Just a few lines to let you know Virginia arrived safely and
seems to have settled in already. It is lovely to have her,
and I have told her she must stay as long as she wants to.
I agree with you that she is much too thin and doesn't look
at all well, but I feel sure the air out here, and the change
of scenery, as well as the eggs and cream and everything
we get from the Fishers (you probably remember Queenie*

*Berry, well she married one of the Fishers from Duck River
and they have a big farm not far from here in the Back
Woods, and their cows and poultry are extremely good),
these things will make all the difference. I have even had
an idea that she might like to help Eva out in the Bluebird,
and that would give Virginia an interest, as Eva is getting
a lot of visitors coming out here at the weekends these days.
They drive in from Woodpecker Point, and also come on
the train. And of course things really pick up here in the
spring and summer when the Gaiety opens for the season.*

*Spring itself seems to be slow in coming this year, with
no sign of any bulbs coming out yet; but the daffodils under
the chestnuts are a picture when they do come out. I have
put Dulcie's bluebells alongside the path all the way down
to the creek. Your grape hyacinths are of course out by the
front door. And thank you, dear, for the snaps of everybody
you sent with Virginia. Eva is so taken with the one of everybody on the suspension bridge she's asked me if she can
put it up on the wall in the Bluebird. I remember I always
used to be very scared on the suspension bridge and the
time Teresa Green dropped her handbag in the water with
all her love letters from Charley Hope in it. The wall in the
Bluebird is quite a rogues' gallery these days, and you will
remember I gave them a snap of your wedding. How time
flies.*

*Getting back to Virginia who is our main concern at the
moment, you will be pleased to know she came along with
us to the Spring Festival today. She is still rather reserved
and shy but that is only to be expected. At the festival she
met some of the locals, what you might call the town's
characters, and she is getting to know people and getting to
know her way around. Philosopher Mean is still our most
colourful character (you will certainly recall the series of
lectures he gave throughout the state just after the war
broke out) and he organizes the festival at a very pretty*

place out on the banks of the Welcome.

Because Philosopher is the brains behind it, the festival has a distinctly pagan flavour, but you will be reassured to learn that Father Wrigly is a most enthusiastic patron. So is Rev. North from the Ironbark Methodist. Philosopher has built a small temple called the Eye of God in the clearing at the foot of the hill. You get to it by going down hundreds of steps that have been cut into the side of the hill, which is extremely steep. I always warn people not to wear high heels, but some of the young ones always do and they are sorry afterwards. It's a very picturesque spot and the rhododendrons are absolutely glorious when they come out. The temple is a sort of pyramid with pictures all over it, and the children like it. We had a big picnic and the choir from the school entertained us, as well as the town orchestra. Daisy and Damien are in the choir and the orchestra, and so are the Mean twins. I meant to say Philosopher has an Aborigine's skull enshrined at the temple like a sort of holy relic, and he claims it's the skull of William Lanney. Nobody really knows where it came from or whose it is, but we all humour Philosopher who is harmless enough I daresay, and he can be very entertaining.

Just quietly, between you and me, I thought Queenie's boy, Jack, was quite taken with Virginia, but she didn't give him a second glance. She is, as I said, so very reserved. That is all to the good in my opinion, and I wish Daisy would take a leaf out of her book. We are still thinking of sending Dais to board at the Deloraine convent when she's twelve. It seems to me that if she goes on the way she's going she will end up being completely out of hand. The local school here is all right up to a point, but I think sending a girl like Daisy to Smithton High would be a bad mistake. What do you think about all this? The nuns have just recently put Veronica World in charge of the boarding house at Deloraine, and I believe she is very good. I hadn't realized she had entered. The last I heard of her was when she was Virginia's teacher in grade one or two.

Well, dear, I will have to close now and get on with a few things. I am in the middle of spinning the fleece Mercy sent me last year. I am working on a woollen sculpture. I know it sounds peculiar, but I am knitting a chapel, and there is nothing like fleece from the Midlands for work like this. I hope this finds you and Vincent and the children well. You never did tell me how the little Quinlan boy was getting on, but I see he is thriving in the snaps you sent. Everyone here sends love,

Dawn

Shaking Virginia Up

Brendan O'Day found his niece Virginia very irritating, and he decided that she needed to be unsettled, shaken up, in order to be forced to come to her senses. Brendan looked at Virginia across the breakfast table and he saw she was thin to the point of ugliness. She faintly resembled her mother at the same age, but she was like a pale, faded, milky impression of her mother. It seemed to Brendan that the sunlight from the window behind Virginia passed through Virginia's right cheek, illuminating the bones of her face, almost laying bare her teeth in their sockets. Virginia, Brendan could see, was preoccupied with the problem of how to avoid eating her breakfast, and she had on her face a look of saintly self-denial and smugness.

'I was reading in the paper,' Brendan said, 'about the importance of chewing. Not so much from the point of view of the digestion, but from the point of view of the teeth. Dentists are discovering that children who don't chew their food get a lot of dental problems. I don't mean decay. I mean their teeth, their second teeth that is, start falling out and there's not much you can do about it. Nothing in fact.'

Virginia's expression did not change.

Virginia's Diary Continues

Saturday, 2 September

Dear Diary, my aunt is going to knit me a jumper in a Fair Isle pattern that will be uniquely mine. She explained it all to me, saying she will put in symbols to signify my name and where I come from. This is done in case I am ever lost at sea and washed up on the beach far away from home. Imagine how it would be then:

'The decomposed body of a young woman has been discovered on Rocky Cape in the vicinity of Red Rock. A jersey, almost perfectly preserved, has led detectives to believe that the dead woman is Virginia O'Day, eldest daughter of Dr and Mrs Vincent O'Day of Launceston. The designs in the jersey show a pattern of blue fleur-de-lys alternating with small golden radiant suns. Virginia had been spending the spring months with her uncle and aunt, Mr and Mrs Brendan O'Day, in Copperfield, in the far northwest. Mrs O'Day says she knitted the jersey for her niece herself, incorporating the symbols into the pattern to suggest her niece's name. On the reverse of the jersey Mrs O'Day included a subtle representation of the Cataract Gorge and of the suspension bridge across the South Esk River, as indications that Virginia's place of residence was Launceston. Mrs O'Day said today in some distress that when she knitted the garment the thought of her niece's drowning was the farthest thing from her mind. It is a tradition among the fishermen of the North Sea to have their identity knitted into their jerseys, and Mrs O'Day said she has knitted hundreds of jerseys for her family and her friends, and she said she always has included in the pattern certain designs that will personally identify the wearer. Mrs O'Day added that as far as she knows the accuracy of her use of symbols has never before been tested under such tragic circumstances.

She said, however, that she derived a certain comfort from the fact that her niece was wearing the jersey at the time of her death, and further that she was pleased to have played a vital part in the swift identification of the body. Mrs O'Day said she takes approximately three and a half weeks to complete one of these beautiful individual jerseys, and she can be contacted at her home in Copperfield. She told reporters today that she has decided to dedicate a certain amount of her time over the next two years to the construction of a chapel which will serve as a memorial to her late niece. The chapel, which Mrs O'Day has been designing for some two years already, will be made, in fact, from wool. It is to be knitted from Tasmanian yarns, spun by Mrs O'Day from the fleeces of flocks from the Midlands property of Mrs O'Day's brother. Mrs O'Day hopes to receive permission for the chapel to be built in one of the prehistoric caves at Woolnorth Point.

One cave in particular was a favourite haunt of Virginia's, a place where she spent many solitary hours, and where she discovered a series of Aboriginal rock carvings hitherto unknown. If application to locate the chapel in the cave is successful, the cave will become a place of pilgrimage, and a site to which people will go to seek the peace and silence that only wild nature can give. The mouth of the cave faces out onto the turbulent waters of Bass Strait, and Mrs O'Day said that the changing moods of the waves always serve to remind her of her own mortality and of the majesty

and awesome dignity of God. When completed, the
chapel will be large enough to hold a priest and two
members of his congregation. Mrs O'Day said she
was inspired to begin designing the chapel when she
read a story of a hermitage made from the bones and
skins of goats on a remote island in the Outer Heb-
rides. A rosary which belonged to the dead woman
will be knitted into the fabric of the east wall of the
chapel, and Mrs O'Day said she plans to unravel a pair
of her niece's gloves and to incorporate the yarn into
the lintel above the door. "By such means Virginia's
own prayers will continue to rise from earth to heaven
through the medium of the chapel dedicated to her
memory," Mrs O'Day said.'

You may think, Dear Diary, that my love of inven-
tion has carried me away, but I must tell you that my
aunt did tell me she is going to knit a chapel, and that
she wants to put it in one of the caves out at Woolnorth. She said she thought I might be interested in
some of the carvings on the rocks, and so we are going
to have a picnic or something out there one day soon.
Food again.

My aunt has a room called a breakfast room, and
we all sat down for breakfast there. I was scared about
the food and how I would avoid it. I knew that if the
worst came to the worst and I had to eat, I could make
myself sick afterwards, but you know I hate doing
that. I was sitting next to Daisy and everybody talked
all the time and ate mountains of cereal and eggs and
bacon and toast and jam so that I could easily have
become hypnotized by the whole thing. Luckily, the
noise and confusion was so great that I managed to
eat nothing at all, and actually Daisy obliged me by
eating a few things I passed on to her. It is a long time
since I sat down to a meal at the table, and never at

such a vigorous table. At the end when there was a triangle of toast on my plate, Uncle Brendan said if I wasn't going to eat it he would eat it, and he picked it up and winked at me. At least I think he was winking at me. He isn't very nice. Jean-Jacques who is only four but considerably brighter than Doll asked me if I was ever going to eat food again. My aunt told him not to ask personal questions, and he said he thought I would die, and everybody laughed like mad so that I hardly knew where to look.

After breakfast we went to a festival for the beginning of spring. It was a funny thing, half religious and half not. It was organized by Bedrock and Carrillo's grandfather who has white hair, quite long like a wizard or a prophet. He has a lovely, kind voice. My aunt said he was christened Philosopher after Philosopher Smith who was the person who first found the copper here. The festival was in a glade at the foot of a very steep slope beside a small river. They have a strange little pyramid there with a sort of holy relic in the form of an Aborigine's head in a glass dome, something like the domes you see in graveyards with china flowers in them. Or domes with clocks under them. We had a picnic but once again, I was able to avoid the food. There were hymns and songs and some children danced and an orchestra played arrangements of folk songs. All this was pretty awful.

Afterwards we went to the Palace Hotel. You would not imagine, Dear Diary, that such a thing as the Palace could exist in this remote little town. Years ago, of course, this place was very rich and quite important, but the copper is becoming more and more difficult to mine and people are moving away. The Palace is small but so grand and glamorous with red velvet and gold fringes and brass mirrors and crystal. I have nev-

er seen such beautiful lights or so many. Even in the
plain bar at the front where the miners drink, there
are hundreds of pretty lights. Daisy said that in the
rooms upstairs where the family live everything is just
ordinary. On the end of the verandah there is a lovely room made from mostly glass, like a conservatory
where they have orchids. I think that room is so beautiful, and I am sad that the conservatory at home is no
longer filled with plants but has become a storeroom
for old and broken things that have not found their
way into the cellar.

I was standing in the parlour bar where everything
is dark red and I was pretending to drink a glass of
lemonade when a boy came up and stood next to me
and started talking. He said he was Jack Fisher from
the Back Woods.

Sunday, 3 September

I thought there would be a fuss when I said I wasn't
going to mass but nothing happened. When they all
came home we had a big Sunday dinner which was
torture for me and simply terrible. I could not escape
and I had to sit next to Uncle Brendan who was at the
head of the table. Luckily Daisy was on my left. The
smell of the roast lamb made me want to be sick and
we had about ten sorts of vegetables. My uncle served
me one slice of meat. I took tiny helpings of some of
the vegetables while everybody else ate like a horse.
I resent the way Uncle Brendan takes command of
every situation. He said, as he was serving my pudding, that people who were thinking of their figures
wouldn't want very much pie, and then he gave me a
small helping and I had to eat nearly all of it. He keeps
looking at me as if he can see exactly what I am think-

ing. I nearly cried right there at the table. I was sick afterwards, but I hate it when I have to do it that way, and now I feel so fat.

My aunt is quite slim; I don't know how she manages that.

On the table was a pink glass sugar caster, and my uncle sprinkled a great shower of sugar onto his pudding. I have never seen anyone eat so much sugar all at once. It sat on the top of his pie like snow. They seem to have a lot of sugar here. On the table there is always a bowl of sugar lumps with silver tongs and Jean-Jacques is allowed to sit there eating the sugar. He is rather round, and yet his teeth appear to be perfect. I am still cleaning my teeth at least seven times a day even though I don't eat anything. My serious fasting has not interfered with my timetable as far as my teeth are concerned.

I realize that my thoughts on such things as teeth and decay and disease and death and so on are probably unusual for a person of my age. I put it down to growing up in a medical household. It must be partly that, in any case. I often read the medical textbooks and I have just remembered some things I read about death by drowning. As you know, I remember these things by heart, and this one is to do with drowning and the contents of the stomach. I am thinking of how it would be if I drowned at Rocky Cape. It said in the textbook: 'In a body which has died from drowning, the lungs and air passages are filled with a fine froth. There is water in the stomach, and the lungs "balloon" with the additional pressure upon them. At the same time the characteristic "clutching at straws"—or indeed sand or paper or anything floating by—may occur. Normally human fat is semi-fluid, but when a body is immersed for a long period in water the fat gradually converts to a condition known as adipocere, a hardening of the fat into a sort of suet condition, which is permanent when complete.' I like to think that if I ever did drown and stay in the water for a long time I would have so little fat on my body I would not turn to suet. Suet is one of the most horrible substances I have ever seen.

'The body of the young woman which was washed up at Rocky Cape had undergone virtually no adipocere change owing to the almost total absence of fat in life. The coroner said, "If this girl has been in the water for the length of time suggested by the weight of evidence, I am inclined to suggest she had been subjected to a rigorous programme of starvation prior to death. I support this theory with further evidence that the stomach of the deceased was in fact in a remarkably shrunken state, and was completely empty of food." Relatives of the deceased are being questioned concerning the young woman's diet and eating habits over the past year and a half.'

Everywhere I go I am surrounded by people who seem to think of nothing but food. The same could be said of me, of course, but in a different way. In the afternoon two of my aunt's friends came to talk about a big cookery book they are doing for the Country Women's. I had to go over to the Bluebird Café with them and my aunt for afternoon tea. I hate having to go to places where there is absolutely nothing but food, where the whole point of the place is food. The Bluebird is such a place. Yet nobody seemed to mind that I didn't eat there, and I spent most of my time looking at the photos on the wall. Some of the photos are very old, and there is even one that is supposed to be Garabaldi when he landed on Three Hummock Island in 1853, nearly a hundred years ago. My mother and father are there on their wedding day, and casts of the plays and pantomimes at the Gaiety. I am pleased to say that not one single photo of me is up on the wall.

My aunt's friends are fat women, and they were dressed in a sort of uniform ladies like that wear. They had white shoes and floral dresses and cardigans and pale overcoats with white gloves and awful, awful hats made from artificial leaves. There they sat in a tiny little café in a small bush town at the farthest corner of the farthest corner of the Empire dressed to go to a garden party at Buckingham Palace with handbags containing powder and lipstick and comb and money and hanky and bobby pins. They discussed puddings and sponges and rock cakes as if the fate of the world depended on such things. They asked me to have a scone, but I said I seldom eat between meals.

Although their book is only a cookery book, it is still a book. I have a sort of funny idea that every book is part of a huge, unimaginable thing which is *The Book*. My aunt's cook book and *Savage Paradise* and the Bible and *David Copperfield* are all sections of *The Book*. While I am in Copperfield I will try to get a copy of *David Copperfield* to read. I have read it before, but it seems to be an appropriate thing to read at the moment. There is sure to be a copy in Philosopher Mean's library, and so I hope I can borrow it.

A Fat Woman Writes to Her Sister Who Happens to be F. X. Quinlan's Mother

Dear Mary,

You will be a bit surprised to hear from me again so soon after my last letter but I have just been over to see Dawn about the recipe book and it's going to be a great goingson

*with hints and recipes and so on from all over the place.
Someone on Bruny Island has sent a recipe for some sort of
wine we dont think we can put it in because of temperance
but its a shame dont you think. Why I am writing so soon
is because Dawn has got Margarets girl Virginia stopping
with her and I have never seen anything like it have you
and so I wanted to write straightaway. Have you seen her
Mary is she dying is it a wasting condition or what do you
think? Dawn in her usual way lets on theres nothing the
matter but I can see it with my own eyes and the girl is in
a bad way. What is being done about it nothing as far as I
can tell and Vincent O'Day a doctor himself. She ate nothing when we were at the Bluebird and just moped about
having a look at the things on the wall there is one picture of her mother and father on their wedding looking so
beautiful. She was such a pretty girl wasnt she and he was
always so good looking and everybody had an eye on him
remember Teresa Green. Dawns garden is a sight to see a
little bit of England soon the bulbs will be out and Dawn
always looks on the bright side silvery lining with everything. She seems to think the girl Virginia will brighten up
in no time with the country air and cooking but if you ask
me its the melancholia I've seen it often enough before and I
know. Thankyou for the snaps you sent they came the other day and I see FX is coming on you must be pleased he's
a big boy how are his eyes now after the second operation.
If Vic is coming down here next week remember to tell him
you cross the bridge and you come through Flowery Gully
around to Kellys Crossing and go over the railway line and
keep on the left of it dont go down as far as Eden the road
is too bad it is about seven miles out and then you go down
the lane below Fishers the Back Woods are very wet at this
time of the year tell Vic if he is coming to bring some fenc-
ing poles and a shovel with him.*

Love and all the best,
Kath

The General Store at Copperfield

Next to the Bluebird Café was the general store which was run by Isis O'Day, widow of one of Virginia's uncles who died in the war. From the general store Virginia bought a postcard to send to her mother and father, and another postcard to use as a bookmark. The card for her parents was a picture of Red Rock; the other card was a picture of a group of Tasmanian Aborigines wearing Victorian silk dresses. The women stood staring at the camera like big mournful dolls. They were fat, and unused to wearing the fancy clothes. Among the soaps and ladders and axes and silks of Isis O'Day's shop, Virginia discovered this photograph of a group of people who were in the process of disappearing.

On the postcard to her parents Virginia wrote:

> *I thought you would like this picture of Red Rock. We have not been out there yet, but we are going one day soon. The trip up here was good, but it is a very long way. I am having a good time, and today I went to Auntie Isis's shop to get this card. Did you know there is a photo of you on your wedding in the Bluebird Café? Everybody sends love, and lots of love from me.*

In her diary Virginia wrote:

> My Aunt Isis said she remembered me when I was a baby. I hate it so much when people say that. She added that I had very fat legs. I must say she is thin, and she is full of energy and runs about all the time even when she isn't serving in the shop. She has such bright blue eyes. I got a picture of some Aborigines

in frocks, and they have such round, sad faces. They made me want to rescue them from whatever it was that was making them so sad. They would be dead now of course because the photo is very ancient, and perhaps they were really only wearing those expressions because they were afraid of the camera. I expect they would have been pleased to be dressed up in all that finery. I love Victorian clothes myself. People do get scared of cameras, especially, I believe, primitive people, because they think the camera is going to steal their souls. I have also heard of people who imagine that the camera removes from the body of the subject a fine layer of the subject's surface. If both these things were true, I would have been without a soul since I was very small, and my skin would have to be worn down past the bone.

The shop was quite busy, mostly with the wives of miners coming in with baskets and little children. They all had long conversations with my Aunt Isis who seems to know everything about everybody who ever lived. It is very useful for a novelist to listen to these things and so I just kept sifting through the cards and eavesdropping on all the conversations. People talk mostly about dull things like the price of sugar or blankets, or about the details of the tragic or wicked things they know about other people. I heard people start off by saying the weather was fine, and they were well, and the child nextdoor was over the measles but still wetting the bed and suffering from suspected kidney disease. Or the weather was fine and the family was well but the woman across the street was drinking too much and beating her children and somebody else's husband had run off to Hobart and was never coming back. They would talk about weddings and babies, and I would think that at last they were going

to have unspoiled and joyful conversations, but before long they would be describing the problems of
the labour or the clashing colours of the bridesmaids'
dresses. It occurred to me as I listened to the women in
the shop that people are always searching for the flaw,
the mistake, the crack in the surface of everything. I
even heard two women talking about Father Moloney
and one of them convinced the other that when he got
up on the table to change the light globe he had been
drinking and that was why he fell.

An odd thing about this place is that I haven't seen
a set of scales anywhere. I thought my aunt would
have some in the shop, but I looked everywhere and
I couldn't see any. I will have to begin a secret search
of Auntie Dawn's house because somewhere she must
have her scales tucked away, and of course I don't dare
ask for a thing like that. Uncle Brendan makes occa-
sional pointed references to the fact that I am thin.
When he does that I feel fatter than ever.

I was invited over to the Palace to see the library,
and I must say I was very surprised and pleased.
When I saw the library I was reminded of a story my
father told me. He had gone to see a patient who lived
on a tiny farm near Scottsdale and he found that every
wall in the house except for the walls in the bathroom
was completely lined with books. The people were
English people who came out here after the war and
brought with them a piano and thousands and thousands of books. The house was small to begin with, but
by the time the man had put up all the bookshelves
everywhere there wasn't much space left in the middle to put the furniture. Perhaps there are houses and
towers containing nothing but books in remote wild
places all over the island. The Means said I can go to
the library whenever I like; they are very kind. There's

a lot of history and philosophy and science as well as novels in the library, and there doesn't seem to be a special order. Sister Patrick who was the library nun at school would have a fit if she saw the way the books are all so higgledy-piggledy.

I sat in one of the armchairs in the library and everything was so peaceful and so cosy and smelling of books I felt as if I was going into a trance. I wanted to read and read and read and write and write and write. I looked out the window and I could see jagged hills covered with dark forest trees. The sun was shining on the trees and yet I thought they looked grim and even menacing. Behind the forest somewhere is the sea.

Mrs Mean brought me a cup of tea and a biscuit and stayed to talk to me. She said *The Old Curiosity Shop* was one of her favourite books and she told me about how the people in Hobart used to wait impatiently for the ships to come bringing the latest books by Charles Dickens from England. I knew she was waiting to see what I would do with the biscuit and so I nibbled the edges. Then after a while the whole biscuit was gone. The strange thing is I am not nearly as upset as I would have expected to be, but I must say I imagined Uncle Brendan (who is in actual fact over at the mine all day) watching me from a secret compartment in the stone wall of the tower. I could imagine his little piggy eye peering through a crack when he saw me begin to nibble. He lurks in the secret place behind the wall until I have eaten the whole biscuit and then he rushes down to the Palace and shouts to all the people that the fast has been broken; the drought has ended; the rivers will flow in the parched and searing desert; the princess has laughed; the sin is original, the niece will toe the line.

When Mrs Mean had gone I started reading *The Mystery of Edwin Drood*.

It was funny to see the first two sentences of the book because they are sentences I could easily have said when I saw the library tower in the grounds of the Palace Hotel. The tower looks so strange and out of place. 'An ancient English Cathedral Tower?' it says at the beginning of *Edwin Drood*. 'How can the ancient English Cathedral Tower be here!' In the story the words are in the mind of a man who is waking up in an opium den, and the solid picture of the tower is followed by scenes from the man's imagination which gives rise to ten thousand scimitars flashing in the sunlight and thrice ten thousand dancing-girls strewing flowers, followed by white elephants. I thought all this was quite unexpected in something called *The Mystery of Edwin Drood* which sounds so sombre. I chose to read *Edwin Drood* first because it has a special kind of fascination for me, being unfinished. The reader is left to imagine the ending. I cannot help being affected by the thought that Charles Dickens died before he completed this book.

But I am puzzled by the book because of the names of many of the characters. They often seem to be such silly names, names that would belong in a pantomime. The heroine is called Rosa Bud, and I don't know how to take that seriously. The orphans are called Landless, and there's a person called Miss Tinkleton, a minor canon called Mr Crisparkle, and there's a Mr Honeythunder. I think these names are funny, but I don't know how funny they are meant to be. The descriptions are beautiful: 'A monotonous, silent city, deriving an earthy flavour throughout from its cathedral crypt, and so abounding in vestiges of monastic graves, that the Cloisterham children grow small salad in the dust of abbots and abbesses, and make dirt pies of nuns and friars.' Every now and again I look up at the picture of Charles Dickens with his little characters floating in the air and I imagine him gently moving them aside. He takes up his pen to describe Rosa Bud eating Turkish Delight which she calls Lumps of Delight. She takes off and rolls up a pair of little pink gloves, like rose leaves, and occasionally puts her little pink fingers to her rosy lips to remove the Dust of Delight that has come off the Lumps. I thought that was a most astonishing and repulsive description of a girl. It isn't just because it refers to eating that I find it sickening; I think it is just creepy, and yet absurd. I delight in such little descriptions as 'a scolding landlady slapped a moist baby (with one red sock on and one wanting).'

The twins, Helena and Neville Landless, remind me of Bedrock and Carrillo, except for the colour of their hair. They are 'an unusually handsome and lithe young fellow, and an unusually handsome lithe girl, much alike, both very dark and rich in colour; she of almost the gipsy type; something untamed about them both; a certain air upon them of hunter and huntress; yet withal a certain air of being the objects of the chase, rather than the followers. Slender, supple, quick of eye and limb; half shy, half defiant; fierce of look; an indefinable kind of pause coming and going on their whole expression, both of face and form, which might be likened to the pause before a crouch or a bound.' It could describe Bedrock and Carrillo, but perhaps twins always look a bit like that. Nobody talks like that any more though. Helena is the opposite of Rosa in some ways; Helena is not afraid of the terrible Jasper, but Rosa faints from fear. I have tried to find Helena and Rosa in the air around Charles

Dickens in the picture, but I do not believe they are there. What I wonder is, if a writer can create Helena, how could he bear to create Rosa.

Dear Diary, I wish I could talk to Charles Dickens about writing novels. And as a matter of fact, any living novelist is just about as remote from me as he is. Once when I was little I wrote a letter to Enid Blyton, but I never got a reply. I remember that I thought at the time I might as well have written to a dead person. I have decided to write a sort of letter to Charles Dickens.

Mr Charles Dickens

Dear Sir,

I have recently come to stay with relatives in the town of Copperfield which is on the far north-west coast of the island of Tasmania. I will be spending much of my time here in the library of a friend, Mr Philosopher Mean. In this library are all your books bound in leather, and there is also a lovely painting of you sitting in your chair with many of your characters floating in the air around you. I have been reading The Mystery of Edwin Drood *and I must tell you that the sound of the name Drood echoes my feelings because I am moody and drooping and brooding.*

I should explain to you that I am not simply a reader and a student of writing, but an aspiring writer.

As I read The Mystery of Edwin Drood *my mind kept returning to thoughts of you, the creator of the novel. I somehow summoned the courage to write to you in this way, and I hope I am not being troublesome. I tried to imagine how the writing of* The Mystery of Edwin Drood *must have fitted into your life. And then I imagined how my unwritten books will fit into my life.*

When I wrote the words 'my life' I saw at once that I should try to describe to you my life which is, I must warn you, practically non-existent. I am seventeen years old and I live on the island of Tasmania in the south-east of Australia. This is the island which used to be called Van Diemen's Land. The old name will certainly mean something to you because of your interest in the lives and fates of prisoners. Van Diemen's Land was first populated by white people because they were looking for a safe place to put their convicted criminals as far away from England as possible. Because of this, our island was, for a long time, a very, very sad place. I have always been struck by the name 'Diemen' which is so close to the word 'demon', and by the presence, in the subsequent name, 'Tasmania' of the word 'mania'. The names evoke a demon madness that I am inclined to think is present here.

One of my ancestors and four of his brothers were sent here from Cork for setting fire to a house and several barns. This part of the history of my family is never mentioned and is a complete secret and a source of dreadful shame. If my father knew I was revealing this to you he would probably kill me. You may wonder how he could do this, and you may consider that I am being fanciful when I say that he would wall me up in the cellar of our house. The ancestor of whom I write was Martin O'Day and he was a well-behaved prisoner and was pardoned and given a grant of land on which he eventually built a lovely house called Goodwood, and where he raised sheep. Although my family are ashamed of him, I wish he had been a more colourful convict. I wish he had been one of the ones who escaped and became a bushranger like Matthew Brady. The bushrangers were more romantic than the convicts who behaved themselves and became respectable. What do you think?

I may say I have never revealed all this to anybody before. It occurs to me that it is even possible my father and other members of the family don't even know about it. In my family there is nobody who shows the same interest in the past as I do. You will wonder how I know the secret myself. When I was twelve we went to Hobart for a holiday. While I was there I spent a lot of time in the museum, and in some old faded documents I read the names of a group of prisoners who arrived here from Cork in 1820. Their names were listed: Martin, Matthew, Thomas, Joseph and James O'Day. These were the names of my ancestor and his brothers. It had to be them. Their crime was also listed. I was shocked but excited and secretly pleased. Our stuffy and respectable present is terribly dull, and I was thrilled to learn of some action and daring in our past. I should explain that my father is a surgeon and my uncle with whom I am staying in Copperfield is the manager of the copper mine. I have other uncles who are lawyers and town councillors. One uncle I have never met, and who is never discussed, is a hermit and probably an alcoholic who lives in a hut at a disused tin mine at a place called Weldborough. I believe he used to share the hut with a Chinese woman but she died.

My grandfather once told me that Martin was given the land at Westbury, where he built Goodwood, in 1825. Then I read in a book at the library that two ex-prisoners were granted land in the Westbury district in that year. So it all fits. There is a nice thing I know about Goodwood: they used to keep peacocks there as watchdogs, and the peacocks were very effective when bushrangers or blacks tried to raid the farm. So that was a rather romantic episode from my family's past. However, the present is truly dull and stifling. My father wants me to become a schoolteacher, but I would rather die. I want to write, and by great good luck I have the chance to spend my days in the library where I can write and read. I have decided to make a study of your work—not only because I admire and enjoy it very much, but because I hope that my reading of your writing will somehow instruct me and inspire me in my own work.

I loved the first paragraph of The Mystery of Edwin Drood *so much I copied it into my commonplace book. And I copied also the second paragraph of chapter three where you mention the children who grow small salad in the dust of abbots and abbesses. You have observed so much, and you have such an exciting way of describing what you have observed. You invented so many ways of doing things in your novels, and I know that I will also have to invent new ways. Many of your characters have become household words so that 'Scrooge', for instance, is a synonym for 'miser'.*

I have so much to read and so much to reflect on, and so much, of course, to write. I am longing for the day when I can hold my own book in my hand. When that day comes I will most certainly send a copy to you.

I am yours sincerely,
Virginia O'Day

Some Sad Stories About Girls

When Virginia had finished writing her letter to Charles Dickens she sat for a long time staring out the window of the tower. Rain was falling. Beneath a grey sky, Virginia could see the dark wet gloom of the myrtle forest on the mountain side. She tried to imagine that as she sat in her chair in the library she was like Charles Dickens, half asleep in his chair, surrounded by the floating figures of characters from stories. She thought of the people she would create in *Savage Paradise* and saw herself with these people dancing in a cloud around her. Would they dance there before she had written them? Perhaps they would not.

Virginia took up her pen and sucked the end of it as she continued to stare out the window. Her notebook was on her knee, but Virginia wrote nothing. Then, uninvited into her mind came the words, 'The trouble is, I am a girl.' It was not like a thought; it was a sentence; a sequence of words; a piece of meaning that seemed to float into Virginia's mind. She said the words aloud: 'The trouble is, I am a girl.' She felt suddenly tearful and forlorn, engulfed in the thick misty greyness of the tower inside and the rain beyond the window. She was alone and helpless, in a trap she suddenly saw as her own nature. She was imprisoned because she was a girl; her gaolers were men: her father, her uncle, Philosopher Mean, Charles Dickens. She began to wonder for the first time who were the women in the lives of Martin, Matthew, Thomas, Joseph and James O'Day. She realized she had never heard of these women; they had been left out of the story altogether. 'The trouble is, I am a girl, and girls don't really count. I am the handmaid of the Lord.'

Dear Diary, I feel like a doll. Once I saw a doll in a museum; it was Elizabeth Batman's doll, lying in a glass case, worn, forlorn, alone, wearing a red velvet bonnet. She was in the glass case with a harpoon gun, a muzzle-loading revolver, a walking stick, a telescope, a holder for a clay pipe, and a silver spectacle case. Some of these things belonged to John Pascoe Fawkner and some belonged to Edward Henty. She lay like a corpse in crimson bonnet and shoes, and her dress was worn cream silk and her arms were made from leather, although her head was wood. There was one other thing in the glass case with her and that was the deed signed by John Batman when he acquired the site of Melbourne from the Aborigines. People who looked at the things in the glass case were expected to know who John Batman and Edward Henty and John Pascoe Fawkner were, but because nobody would know anything about the owner of the doll, there was a notice in the glass case about her. It said she was John Batman's daughter and she died of a softening of the brain.

I feel like the doll in the glass case with the harpoon gun and the revolver. And I believe I have realized, Dear Diary, that my way out of the glass case, my way out of the trap is through writing. It isn't just that I want to write; I *have* to write. I will have to learn to use words like tempered steel to cut my way out. I have always been very uncomfortable about the endings of stories such as 'Sleeping Beauty' and 'Snow White' and I have realized that this is because the girls remain powerless to the last. Snow White lies in her glass coffin until she is rescued by the kiss of the prince; and Sleeping Beauty can only be released from sleep by the prince who destroys the forest of thorns and kisses her. If I can't get out of my own glass coffin, through my own forest, I would rather be dead. I don't know how I am going to do this, and it isn't going to be easy, but I am going to try. I have felt so oppressed for so long now, and I have finally realized that it is just because I am a girl. I wish I could be like Bedrock and Carrillo who are two parts of the one person, boy and girl, but that is a vain and foolish wish. I have heard that everybody starts out by being a twin, but usually one twin dies long before it is time to be born.

I will write *Savage Paradise,* and I want also to write a story about Mathinna. In my father's surgery there is a print of a portrait of Mathinna and this portrait and the life of its subject have haunted me for a long time. First of all, Mathinna, an Aboriginal girl, was named Mary by her own people, but English people called her Mathinna. In her case the common practice of re-naming the blacks with English names was reversed. Mathinna had a sister, however, who was called after George Augustus Robinson, and she was known as Mr Robinson's Duke.

Mathinna was taken away from her own family when she was five years old. She went to live at Government House in Hobart with Governor and Lady Franklin and their family. The Franklins had a daughter named Eleanor, and Mathinna shared Eleanor's governess. When Mathinna was seven she had her portrait painted, wearing her red dress. The print my father has in the surgery is of this portrait. Lady Franklin sent the portrait to her sister in England with a letter: 'She always wears the dress you see her in. When she goes out, she wears red stockings and black shoes.'

Eleanor copied into her diary a letter Mathinna wrote to Governor Franklin when she was six. I saw the diary and copied out the letter myself: 'Mathinna is six years old. Her mother Eveline, father, modern name Hannibal, Cape Sorell tribe. I am good little girl. I have pen and ink cause I am good little girl. I do love my father. I have got a doll and shift and a petticoat. I read. My father I thank thee for sleep. I have got red frock. Like my father. Come here to see my father. I have got sore feet and shoes and stockings and I am very glad.'

I think the story is already very sad, but it gets much worse. When the Franklins returned to England, Mathinna, who was used to the life at Government House, was sent to live at the Queen's Orphan School in Hobart. Then afterwards she was sent to the Aboriginal settlement on Flinders Island. She was eight then. Later on she was returned to the Orphan School where she and five hundred other children lived in overcrowded rooms and were listless and very unhappy. When Mathinna was sixteen she left the school to go to the forlorn Aboriginal settlement at Oyster Cove. She seemed from that time to give up all hope, and when she was twenty-one she fell into a puddle in the darkness after drinking too much, and drowned.

Long before I ever knew the story of Mathinna's life I used to look at the picture of Mathinna in my father's surgery. The girl in the picture looked so sweet and wistful and fragile and I often used to think about her and wonder what her life was like. I never imagined anything like the truth. I would sometimes go up the dry hillside on the other side of the Gorge. I remember I used to call the Gorge 'the gorgeous Gorge of the gorgon'. I would take my lunch with me in those days when I was a fat little girl, and a book to read, and I would cross the King's Bridge and go up the steep and dangerous Zig-Zag Path. I loved the name of that path, and the path itself was so rocky and barren. But often the names of places in Launceston are royal and so it seems as if a little family of kings and queens must have lived there. We have the Prince's Square, the Royal Park, the Albert Hall, and many places called George and Elizabeth, as well as the Queen Victoria Museum. When I got to the Giant's Grave, which is a huge jutting boulder, I would sit down and have my lunch and read my book.

Far below me was the troubled water of the Gorge, and the wet hillside on the other side of the water was dark with thick wet trees. It looked, from where I was, like a place of menace and mystery. I imagined that the path snaking along the side of the wet hillside was a primitive track. There in the shadows flitted Mathinna in her red dress and stockings. She danced and ran from cave to cave beneath the feathery fronds of cool, damp ferns. Like a ladybird she settled, tiny, on the petal of an orchid; then she spread her wings to the wind and quickly flew away into a place where I could no longer see her. I screwed up my eyes and shaded them with my hand. I saw her again. She was far, far away from me across the yellow frothy water and I saw her as she appeared and disappeared in the dewy half-light and dripping gloom of the rocks and the ferns. A dragonfly-girl, she flashed in and out of the darkness like a ruby, like a garnet, like a fish, bright crimson, like a flittering firetail.

(You hear of people committing suicide by 'jumping over the Gorge', but I have never heard of an actual person who did it. When you say it—'jumping over the Gorge'—it sounds as if you stand on top of either the wet hill or the dry hill and then you leap off into space and land in the water. But if you tried that you would always, as far as I can see, land on rocks; you would never get to the water. You could jump from the King's Bridge, but unless you carried a bag of stones, or better still had stones in your pocket like Virginia Woolf, you probably wouldn't drown.)

The place where I used to sit dreaming about Mathinna was a boulder called the Giant's Grave, but some people knew it as Brady's Lookout. It seems to me that whenever they find a big jutting rock on top of a high hill in Tasmania (and they often do) they imagine Matthew Brady there, hunted and watching for soldiers, and they call it Brady's Lookout. I sat on the Giant's Grave and I imagined Mathinna playing forever in the shadows on the opposite hill.

The Gorge of the Gorgeous Gorgon

It was forty years after Virginia wrote those words in her diary that she was welcomed back to her home town to write a play celebrating the existence of the Historic Museum Village of

Copperfield. She was taken for a ride in a Fly-By-Nite helicopter by the Mayor. The pilot of the Fly-By-Nite was F. X. Quinlan who said he remembered Virginia from when she lived next to his family.

'Once you got cockroaches in you ears,' FX said to Virginia.

'Not the sort of thing one cares to recall,' the Mayor said with a smile.

In the place where her home used to be, Virginia saw the glass dome of the village beneath which twinkled a million bright white lights. Virginia saw the blue of the lighted swallow, and she said, 'Oh look, that must be the Bluebird Café.'

BOOK THREE ·
THE INTERVIEWS

The only Paradises are lost Paradises.

Samuel Beckett, *How It Is*

Interview one

The parlour at the Palace Hotel in the Historic Museum Village was a charming replica of the parlour at the old Palace. It was furnished in rich comforting shades of dark red. When Virginia went to Launceston as the guest playwright for The Best People, she stayed at the Palace and journalists came to the parlour to interview her. Modern comforts had been added to the authentic nostalgia of the Palace, and although the whole hotel was centrally heated by electricity, a fire always burned in the parlour grate except in the very height of summer. It was a replica of the fire into which Bedrock Mean had cast the crumpled letter left in the bedroom by Nancy Best.

'I left the island in 1953 and I have not been back since then,' Virginia said to the journalists. 'I remember coming back from Copperfield where I had just spent nearly three years before going overseas. During those three years I completed a novel, *Savage Paradise.* No, it has not been published but it is going to be published this year in New York. It's a love story set in Tasmania in the early part of last century. The sort of thing the Americans find quite interesting. It is very much a young girl's fantasy of what life was like in the early days of the colony, romantic, but I believe it gains something for being like that. The main character, Elizabeth, reminds me of what I think I was like, and the things that happened in the story are things I used to think I wanted to happen to me. Yes, I'm glad they didn't happen. She is brave and beautiful and resourceful and has all kinds of dangerous adventures with convicts and horses and Aborigines and floods and childbirth. She marries the matching man from the neighbouring property of course, and they live more or less happily ever after. No, giving away the plot won't stop people from reading it. Everybody knows all the plots, don't they?'

Interviewer: If everybody knows all the plots, why do you think people keep reading books?

Virginia: Perhaps it's very reassuring to keep being told the same things in different ways. And every storyteller puts the story together in a different way. It's nice to see how it's done each time. You can arrange plenty of surprises for the reader.

Interviewer: How did you feel when you read the final proofs of *Savage Paradise* which you wrote so long ago?

Virginia: I felt as if I was looking through a window into a room where there was a mirror, and in the mirror I could see the reflection of a photograph on the wall, and the photograph was a picture of a window in which I saw the reflection of a girl.

Interviewer: It sounds as if you might have been the girl.

Virginia: I might have been. I was thinking also of the old Bluebird Café where I wrote a fair bit of the book. When you looked in the window there you could see part of the wall of photographs reflected in the mirror on the sideboard. I suppose if I look in the window of the Bluebird down the street I'll see the same thing. I must remember to look.

Interviewer: You wrote some of the novel in the old Bluebird Café in Copperfield; where else did you write it?

Virginia: In several different places. I remember I began to write it one day when I was about seventeen. I used to go to the old cemetery above the Chinese market garden. I don't suppose any of that sort of thing exists now. I would go and sit in one of the ruined sepulchres and look right out across the valley and down the river, and I would feel, I think, that I was in a safe place where I could write whatever I wanted to write. It was the old Scotch cemetery and the characters in the story all come from Scotland, the main characters, that is. I imagined I was sitting on Elizabeth's grave.

Interviewer: Those graves were like small chapels; so sitting there must have been rather like sitting on a doorstep.

Virginia: Yes, now you mention it, it was just like that.

Interviewer: You spoke earlier of windows and now of doors; images of windows and doors seem to come up frequently in your fiction. Is this a conscious motif that you are exploring?

Virginia: It isn't conscious in the sense that I sort of think, oh, it's time I put in some doors and windows. It is more spontaneous and unconscious than that. But when I start writing about a window or a door (I think there are more windows than doors) I have the thought quite soon that I have come to a lovely part in the story where I can think about windows again.

Interviewer: Why do windows interest you so much?

Virginia: I am fascinated by boundaries, where one thing ends and another begins. A window is a transparent skin dividing one world from another, and it is also a frame through which one world can look into another. Windows are places of hope and possibility. They let the light in. When I was a child I went to the ruined prison at Port Arthur and I let them shut me for about half a minute in the solitary confinement cell where no light at all was permitted to enter. Perhaps that made me long for windows forever after; I don't know. I am also interested in the place where the land meets the water, particularly when there are cliffs.

Interviewer: In a sense you grew up on the top of a cliff, didn't you?

Virginia: Yes, I did. On top of this very cliff where we are now. In fact, I must try to work out where our old house would have been.

Interviewer: The Best People could probably tell you that.

Virginia: I must remember to ask.

Interviewer: We are in the parlour of the Palace Hotel. How does it compare with the parlour of the old Palace, as you recall it?

Virginia: It seems to me that it looks almost exactly the same; the same red lights, velvet curtains, red velvet seats and chairs; and the fireplace is an exact replica.

Interviewer: I believe it *is* the same fireplace.

Virginia: That explains it. But I must say, that although this parlour *looks* like the old parlour, it *feels* different. I believe that rooms that have been used for a long time are sort of inhabited by the things that have happened in them. Nothing has really happened here; it's an imitation. The same thing applies in the buildings in theme parks all over the world.

Interviewer: They always say this isn't a theme park.

Virginia: Whatever it is, it was manufactured; it was put here not because there was a copper mine but because there were tourists. And I can assure you that it feels not like Copperfield, but like Disneyland. How could it feel like anything else? The Best People would probably be the first to say so; after all, the Historic Museum Village is here to entertain people. The fact that it is like a great big snow dome is a matter of some interest to me, actually. It's like a childhood dream come true and gone mad on an enormous scale. I used to have a collection on snow domes when I lived here; I had dozens of little captive worlds where I could shake the snow and cause this dreadful turbulence; then the flakes would settle again and the trees and people and things under the dome would be there bright and still just the way they were before. A couple of the domes had loose pieces that had broken off so that the figures floated and wandered around and would never stay in the place where they were meant to be. I had a floating baby Jesus and a floating tower of Pisa.

Interviewer: You were speaking earlier about the places where you wrote *Savage Paradise.* Do the places where you write have an effect on your work?

Virginia: I think they sometimes do. I have written in planes and hotel rooms and railway stations, and even those places, I suppose, have some sort of effect on the writing. But when I was writing this first book I think I had a romantic notion about being an artist and following my art in places that fed my imagination. Now I come to think of it, I was probably right about some of that. As I said, I began the novel in the ruined cemetery, and I certainly did derive inspiration from my surroundings. Then I wrote a great deal of the book in the old Charles Dickens Library in Copperfield. This library is reproduced behind the hotel. If you look out the side window over there you can see it, the tower. Philosopher Mean used to let me go there and read and write.

Interviewer: What sort of things did you read?

Virginia: I read the works of Dickens, starting at *Edwin Drood* and working backwards to *Pickwick.*

Interviewer: Why did you do it that way, backwards?

Virginia: I have sometimes wondered whether I had a sound reason, or whether I just did it that way to be different. At the time I thought it would be somehow instructive to follow a writer's development from the end to the beginning.

Interviewer: And was it?

Virginia: Hard to say. I probably would have learnt just as much by doing it randomly or from the beginning to the end.

Interviewer: Why did you do it at all?

Virginia: There were several reasons: I believed Dickens was a great writer, and I knew I could learn things about writing from his work; then I was actually in a town that I supposed was named in honour of *David Copperfield*; and I was in a library named for the author. I think there seemed to be no question about what I would read. I had read some Dickens before, but at this time I read him obsessively. In fact, I became obsessed with him and his life. I read biographies; I imagined I might be the reincarnation of Ellen Ternan; I wrote letters to Charles Dickens.

Interviewer: I find it a bit hard to believe that you were permitted to spend three years in the country doing these things. How did that happen?

Virginia: When I left school I didn't want to go to university and become a teacher and get married and so on. I didn't even want to grow up; I didn't want any responsibility. I wished to be a child forever, having taken Peter Pan very much to heart. I was terrified of being an adult, of getting old and dying. I was even prepared to die young in a perverse attempt to cheat death. So I began to starve myself. As I talk about it now, all these years later, I may seem to suggest that all this was carefully thought out. A lot of it was thought out, but some of the conclusions about my behaviour at that time are conclusions I have come to over the years. However, when I read my old journals from that time I can see that I was acting in a pretty calculated way.

Interviewer: You still have your old journals?

Virginia: Yes, I have kept a journal more or less consistently since I was young. In fact, the manuscript of *Savage Paradise* was lost, but I was able to reconstruct it last year from the journals.

Interviewer: Was your starving described as anorexia at that time, or what?

Virginia: It was not described as anything, as far as I can remember; it was scarcely referred to. I was just an impossible nuisance, and I was sent to stay with my aunt at Copperfield in the hope that the country air and food and change of scenery and companionship would bring me to my senses. In a way it had the desired effect, but it took a long time. I did come to my senses and start eating and living again. I poured out a lot of my troubles in my letters to Charles Dickens, and I think that helped me to sort things out.

Interviewer: You didn't discuss your troubles with living people?

Virginia: No, I don't think I really trusted anybody very much then. My aunt was very kind and patient, and so was Philosopher Mean. And there was a boy called Jack Fisher who used to bring over the eggs from his family's farm; he started coming up to the library to talk to me. He tempted me with apples, just like Adam and Eve in reverse; lovely little red apples that looked so sweet and crisp. In the end I started eating them, and that was probably the turning point—from then on I gradually came back to life. Once or twice I went to the pictures in Woodpecker Point with Jack, but we didn't have any big romance. Still, I am forever grateful to him for the apples. And for his persistence. I hated and feared my home and my family because I felt confined and crippled by them; and Jack somehow changed my outlook, made me stop twisting and turning in a trap of my own making, and made me take the simple way out which was to start being honest about what I wanted. I started by eating the apple I wanted to eat, and then, after quite some time, you understand, I was able to explain to my aunt and then to my father that I wanted to be a writer, and to go to London and get work and get on with writing. It all sounds so simple now, but it was dreadfully complicated at the time.

Even though I have my journals of that time to read, the truth of how I was and what I felt is sometimes too faded in my memory for me to be able to decipher it. I have great admiration for people who are able to write their autobiographies. It seems to me that I would not know where to begin, where to look for the truth of how things were. But I know that at some time during my stay at Copperfield, some time I am sure after I started eating the apples Jack brought me, I felt my childhood slipping away from me, falling away like an old garment, and I felt myself letting it go. I stopped looking back at it with regret, stopped clinging on. I realize now that my father was trying to show me one easy way of doing this, but I wanted to create my own way, and I finally did.

Interviewer: You have said that you hope to write a play to be performed in the Gaiety; have you decided on a subject?

Virginia: I tried not to think about a subject until I got here. I have had a most interesting time exploring the Historic Museum Village, and I have had several inspirations. What I have kept coming back to, however, is the story of the disappearance of Lovelygod Mean. I think that would make a good play . I read some of the solutions to the mystery that people had proposed at the waxworks. So many of them want to believe that Lovelygod is alive and is going to come back.

Interviewer: What do you think?

Virginia: It seems unlikely to me that Lovelygod would be still alive, but I will do what I nearly always do with a play or a story—I will let the writing take over and solve the problem for me in the context of the work. In a sense, for the sake of the drama, it doesn't matter what really happened; the world of the play will be what matters.

Interviewer: People will believe the play; they will think that what the play says happened really happened?

Virginia: I might find that the play calls for alternative endings where the audience chooses to believe whichever ending they want. Many people believe that Lovelygod never existed.

Interviewer: Do you think she did?

Virginia: Lovelygod really existed; I know that. So do you.

Interviewer: Do you think people will think you are re-opening the case? If she was kidnapped and murdered there may be people still around who would prefer to let sleeping dogs lie.

Virginia: I am only writing a play, not re-opening a case. It seems to me to be a very Australian story, the story of Lovelygod. Children disappear without a trace. My childhood was haunted by the print of a painting we had at home. It was by an Australian painter and showed a small girl in a pink dress lying in the grass beneath a tree, and it was called *Lost.* There was a similar picture in our neighbour's house called *Lost in the Bush* and it had two children in it. Then in our third-grade reader we had that story called 'Lost in the Bush' about some children in Victoria who were lost and then found days later, nearly dead. An interesting thing about that story is that when I have mentioned it to

people who read it as children they have all forgotten that
the children were found. People tell me the children were
never found. The story of *Picnic at Hanging Rock* was taken
to be true, true to the behaviour of the Australian bush.
Perhaps we are ready to believe these things because deep
down we think we don't belong here, and the land itself will
sometimes swallow up our children to punish us.

Interviewer: Some people think Lovelygod was swallowed by
the horizontal forest. What do you think about that?

Virginia: It is certainly possible, but it raises the question of
what was a ten-year-old girl doing out in the horizontal
forest in the middle of the night. It doesn't answer anything
very much.

Interviewer: You knew Lovelygod's parents when they were
young; have you had any contact with them since?

Virginia: Only with her father, Carrillo. He is the head of the
James Barrie Institute for the Recovery of Lost Children, in
Los Angeles.

Interviewer: So Lovelygod's father is still actively searching for
her?

Virginia: I believe the file is still open.

Interviewer: If you do write the play on this subject, will you
dwell on the fact that the child was the product of incest?

Virginia: My principal concern in referring to incest in the
play would be to try to make clear the distinctions between
three factors: the disappearance of the child, the incest of
the parents, and the size of the child. Those three things are

all separate, and yet people often confuse them, making the size of the child dependent on the incest of the parents, and then drawing the conclusion that there is a direct relationship between these factors and the disappearance.

Interviewer: But if Lovelygod was stolen for a circus or for medical research, then there was such a relationship.

Virginia: But not if she was swallowed by the forest or eaten by a Tasmanian Devil. I would choose to separate all three factors in any case.

Interviewer: Did you visit the James Barrie in order to do research into Lovelygod?

Virginia: No, I simply went there to visit Carrillo as someone I had known years ago. He told me most of the cases on file at the James Barrie are Australian, and most of them are girls under the age of twelve. It crossed my mind at that point that the Institute might have been better named after Lewis Carroll, actually, but I refrained from comment. And of course Barrie did have a group of characters called 'the Lost Boys'.

Interviewer: Writers always seem to be so ready with literary references.

Virginia: Yes, we are. And I believe I can see you thinking that my position is that of the cold observer. In some ways it has to be. In order to write a drama on the theme of loss, which is something that touches us all, I need to see things in this way a lot of the time.

Interviewer: You often write about loss of one kind or another.

Virginia: Yes, I do. And you will find that loss is the subject of a great deal of serious writing.

Interviewer: You could see the building of the Historic Museum Village as an attempt to recover a lost town.

Virginia: Yes, it is an attempt at the reconstruction of history, but history is such an elusive matter, isn't it? My play which will be inspired by the tragic disappearance of one little girl will not be an attempt to write history, or to write documentary; it will be an attempt to create a new thing, a play, using as the genesis part of the story of the child.

Interviewer: How would you describe *Savage Paradise*, then, in the present context?

Virginia: That is ninety-nine parts fantasy, and one part, if we are lucky, history. But I must say that when I read the book and remember what was going on in my own life when I was writing it, I am surprised, and cannot see the connection between the two. The conclusion I have come to about all that is that the imagination is a wonderful and even an independent thing. There I was, a rebellious, starving, miserable, disagreeable, self-absorbed adolescent, and yet to read the book you would never guess. The real me was going into my journal and into the letters to Charles Dickens.

Interviewer: You used to write in the Charles Dickens Library and in the Bluebird Café. Do you think you will write the play in those places?

Virginia: Definitely not. I will be writing in the office The Best People have provided for me upstairs.

Interviewer: When did you stop being a romantic?

Virginia: A long time ago.

Interviewer: Perhaps when you ate the apple?

Virginia: Perhaps.

Interview two

Before going into the Bluebird Café, Virginia looked through the window. She saw people sitting at the tables having tea and cakes, and she saw that the photographs on the wall were reflected in the mirror on the sideboard. The place was cosy and inviting; the woman behind the counter even resembled Eva Mean. She had long red hair and moved in a swift but graceful way.

Interviewer: Is this a faithful replica of the old Bluebird?

Virginia: I think it looks just like it, but it doesn't feel like it. The photographs don't seem to be as worn as they used to be. I can see there is one of my parents on their wedding day, and one of my Aunt Isis. Isis had the general store in Copperfield and I remember I surprised her by saying she was named after an Egyptian goddess. It turned out she was named after a Tasmanian river.

Interviewer: It must be very strange for you to come and find the replica of the Copperfield you knew in the place where your own home used to be.

Virginia: It's weird, and I am constantly examining my feelings and my reactions to things. I have discovered that the Bluebird and the general store are built on the place where my family home was. In fact, The Best People bought our house and the Quinlan's house next door and lived there while they were planning to build the Village.

Interviewer: So you and I are sitting in the exact place where you were born.

Virginia: Probably. I was born in the conservatory, and I remember when I was little that the conservatory was always filled with ferns and flowers and I used to play in there. But my parents must have become too busy over the years and they lost interest in the conservatory and it became a place where we kept rusty old bicycles and things. Only once I think it was cleaned out when a psychiatrist from overseas came to stay and he said that he would clean it out if he could sleep in there. So he did. But afterwards all the rubbish, or most of it, went back in. At least he had cleaned the glass. Talking about all this now makes me very sad. I have a sudden and clear understanding that the conservatory is irretrievable.

Interviewer: Would a photograph of the conservatory make you feel better?

Virginia: It might; but it might make me feel worse. Have you seen such a photograph?

Interviewer: Is that it on the wall?

Virginia: No, that would be the conservatory at the Palace Hotel. If there was a picture of ours it would have been in the cellar where my father kept all the negatives and prints of the photographs he took. I believe they didn't clear out the cellar before they pulled down the house to build the village. So I imagine the cellar now as a place where silent, spongy toadstools lurk and puff and spread in murky, damp, colourless folds and clouds, this type feeding on the negatives, that other feeding on the prints. There would be other things left behind and rotting in the cellar, but the photographs are the things I remember most. It was my father's hobby, his passion, photography. My sister said she didn't clear out the cellar when the house was sold. It's a pity.

Interviewer: It happens, doesn't it? I spoke to F.X. Quinlan and he told me his father built a boat in their cellar and they couldn't ever get it out. It was still there when that house was sold, and FX said it was still there when The Best People pulled the house down.

Virginia: Trevallyn is beginning to sound like Sutton Hoo. My uncle in Copperfield was a great boat builder. In fact, my play, *Brendan the Navigator*, was inspired by him and his idea of building a boat and sailing around the world.

Interviewer: It was an idea. Did he ever do it?

Virginia: No; people hardly ever do, do they? In fact, when I came to think about it, I realized my uncle never intended to finish the boat. The whole point was the dream and the building. My aunt was extremely patient; she was very understanding. In fact, she was really the one, I think, who brought me back to my senses. It was she who provided a place for me to stay while I worked things out; and she gave me the freedom to read and write to my heart's content.

Interviewer: Was the woman in your novel *A* inspired by your aunt in Copperfield?

Virginia: She was partly. A character is always, as far as my work is concerned, a complicated fusion of many inspirations; but yes, the character of Lydia was principally inspired by my aunt. Readers have sometimes asked me where the idea came from, of a woman who knits a chapel and places it in a cave where Aborigines used to shelter; well, it came straight from my aunt. She was knitting the chapel when I was living with her in Copperfield. She had a terrific lot of trouble getting permission from the authorities to put the chapel in the cave, but in the end she did it. I think they couldn't stop her really.

Interviewer: Why didn't they want her to do it? Because the land was an old, sacred site of the Aborigines?

Virginia: Oh no, nothing like that; because it was an eccentric idea. The people of Copperfield and Woodpecker Point were generally very conventional, and they tried to check eccentricity whenever they could. My aunt's mistake was in asking for permission. When Philosopher Mean built the Temple of the Eye of God, for instance, he didn't ask; he just went ahead and did it.

Interviewer: It must have been a very religious place.

Virginia: When I was there in the early fifties, people made their own entertainment. They were forever putting on plays and operas and so on at the Gaiety. But much of the entertainment, the festivals, the concerts, the choirs and dances, were organized by the churches and other religious groups. And religion itself, for all its foundation in faith, has always seemed to me to be a form of entertainment. I think all I am saying is that people then didn't have cars and they didn't have television, and so the churches in Copperfield were quite vigorous and important. They also had the

hotels; that hasn't changed. But it wasn't what I would call a
religious place, really.

Interviewer: Would your aunt's chapel still be in the cave?

Virginia: It blew away in a storm and was washed out to sea;
and strangely enough this happened the day before my
aunt died. I find that kind of coincidence interesting; it suggests a real connection between my aunt and her creation.
No such thing happened to Lydia's chapel because I wrote
the book long before my aunt died, and you can't put coin-
cidences like that in fiction and be taken seriously.

Interviewer: Some of your less serious work has been in writing
musical comedy. Will the play about Lovelygod be a serious drama, or will it be closer to your comic writing? Your
play *The Bluebird Café Murders*, for instance, was a suspense
drama, but it was also a comedy.

Virginia: The *Murders* were pure fantasy, and what you say
about the play is true. But the material and the inspiration
for this new play is different—I know the lost child's parents; I remember the conservatory at the end of the Palace
verandah, the room from which she disappeared; she was a
real child who walked on the streets of Copperfield where I
have walked, who bought her comics and barley sugar from
the general store which was a very familiar place to me.

Interviewer: But you never met Lovelygod?

Virginia: No, I never met her, and I am inclined to think that if I
had, I wouldn't be able to contemplate writing this play. As
it is, I plan to write something with the flavour of Maeterlinck's *The Blue Bird*.

Interviewer: Almost children's pantomime?

Virginia: Well, a sort of lyrical drama with music and chorus.
But I don't usually talk about my work in this way before I
have written it. I would just like to say that I feel compelled
to write about Lovelygod, and I am uncertain of the form
the work will take. The noise in here is completely different from the sounds of the old Bluebird Café, by the way.
And the smells; *that's* what's really different; that's what
makes the difference. This place *looks* almost exactly like
the Bluebird, except, as I said before, for a certain newness,
a certain sharpness of the edges. But the smell is what
really gives it away. I noticed the same thing in the general store. The old general store had an absolutely ancient,
ancient smell all of its own. It was sweet and spicy and
mysterious and completely seductive. I used to love to go in
there and just breathe the air. My Aunt Isis was never too
busy to talk; in fact I liked to listen while she talked to the
people who came into the shop. All the history and gossip
of Copperfield could be picked up in the shop and in the
Palace Hotel. I was a great listener. I think I used to get on
people's nerves because I was so silent, and so horribly thin,
of course. I heard things that I remembered for years and
eventually put into my fiction. The woman who insisted
on calling fence-posts fence-poles was somebody I used
to hear speaking to my Aunt Isis. The rhythms of speech
are as distinctive as fingerprints, and I think that woman's
rhythms interested me as much as her subject matter did.
She used to stare at me and I used to listen to her and stare
into the distance.

Interviewer: You have talked about some of the things that have
changed since you lived here; but are there things you see
that are still the same?

Virginia: Not very much. The whole place—I mean the airport, the town and so on, are different in the way they feel. Of course I'm different too. But I went for a walk up the old zigzag path, and I thought that hadn't changed. It was still the same dry, stony, rocky track, and the Giant's Grave was still there. But when I looked down at the Gorge, at the water, everything looked smaller and less significant than I remembered it. I tried to forget the great glass dome on the skyline, and just consider the water and the wet hillside. But of course it's impossible to ignore the dome.

I used to imagine I could see the ghosts of the Aborigines in the darkness of the rocks and ferns across the water. When I was there recently at the Giant's Grave I looked down and tried to imagine the ghosts, but I couldn't. I fancifully imagined that all this activity on top of the hill had chased the ghosts away. The last time I went up the zigzag was thirty years ago.

Something that shocked me in town was the disappearance of the public library. I went there when I was very little with my grandfather, and I felt, when we were going up a spiral staircase, that we were inside a seashell. Light was falling on us through frosted glass, and we were going up, up into the shell in a kind of quiet ecstasy. Perhaps it's just as well for me the library isn't there. It probably wouldn't be like a seashell any more. But what makes me sad is when I try to recover the image of me and my grandfather going up the staircase, I keep thinking of us being like paper dolls, suddenly flattened as the library is erased.

Interviewer: It must be even worse when you think of your home and all the streets and houses around it being knocked down to make way for the Historic Museum Village.

Virginia: No, it isn't worse. I have thought about it a great deal

and I've decided that the removal of the suburb of Trevallyn
is so unimaginable to me that I can't begin to feel about it.
With the library it's just that image of me and my grandfather inside the seashell, but with the place where I grew up,
the disappearance, the total destruction of the place where
I grew up, as if by war or natural disaster, is numbing to
my imagination, and so I can't reach my feelings about it. I
thought that when I got here and saw for myself that everything had gone I would remember and mourn. I can't.

I can speak of only one feeling I have had about all this
since I came back; I was up at the Giant's Grave looking
down at the water and trying to imagine how I used to
imagine an Aboriginal girl in a red dress running in and out
of the ferns on the other side of the Gorge, when I looked
up at the glass dome of the village. The sun was striking it
at such an angle that it seemed for a few moments to be a
vast and terrible jellyfish. What I felt was fear. I am not being very wise or diplomatic in saying these things. When I
was a child I was terrified of all the jellyfish in the water. We
went to the beach every summer, and I hated and feared the
jellyfish—there were always so many—not only because
they would sting me, but because they were silent and
transparent and would just float up to you from nowhere.
My sister Doll was forever being stung by insects and
things, and every day at the beach she would be attacked by
jellyfish and come screaming out of the water with horrible
red welts on her. All this came back to me when I saw the
dome as a jellyfish on the top of the hill. It was just something the sun was doing; it was casting images under the
glass that had the appearance of the spooky, internal stuff
in the jellyfish. It was just a trick of the light.

Interviewer: Have you ever thought that Lovelygod might have
been bitten by a snake?

Virginia: Well, supposing snakes bite in the middle of the night, the question still remains: what was she doing out in the bush, and then there's the matter of the body. No trace, this child disappeared with no trace. It seems to me you are hoping my play will provide an answer to the mystery.

Interviewer: Won't it?

Virginia: I think there are two kinds of stories; there's the kind that answers questions, and the kind that asks them. The ones that answer questions are the simple ones like *Savage Paradise,* for instance. At the end of books like that you are left in no doubt about where the characters came from, where they went, and what happened in between. I am now more interested in stories that ask questions. This play, *Waiting For Lovelygod*, will ask a lot of questions. The main ones are: Did Lovelygod Mean really exist? If she existed how did she disappear? Is she still alive? If not, how did she die? We know she existed, but I believe the play still has to ask the question. I have asked The Best People for access to the solutions people write at the waxworks. I plan to include many different solutions in the drama. The longest and most interesting one was written by a visiting Japanese schoolgirl who claimed that Lovelygod or Lovelygod's ghost spoke to her in a dream. But you will really have to wait until the play is written.

Interview three

The Charles Dickens Library Tower behind the Palace Hotel was built to the dimensions of the original tower in Copperfield, but it seemed to Virginia to be much smaller than the library she remembered.

Virginia: Not a trick of the light but a trick of time and memory. I used to think the library in Copperfield was a vast place, overwhelming in its number of books. I feel as if I am in some toy version of it and yet I know it's the same size. The sad thing is that when I used to look out the window I could see the mountains and the tops of trees and I knew that between me and the sea there was nothing but the bush. From this window I can see the ferris wheel and the pirate ship and thousands of people from all over the world in bright clothes carrying cameras and eating toffee apples on sticks. I'm not really complaining, you understand, just noticing. I have always loved that picture of Dickens sitting in his chair, surrounded by his characters. One of my own propositions about Lovelygod is that she slipped from the twentieth century to become a character in a novel by Dickens. I could just imagine her in that painting, hovering like an ice-blue fairy behind the author's head. Every scene in the play, you see, deals with a different possibility; and all the time Lovelygod's mother waits for her in the Bluebird Café, and her father searches for her with computers.

Interviewer: You are going into more detail about the play than I expected you would.

Virginia: I have begun to enjoy talking about it, and about all the other things. That's an interesting thing about interviews; when I am talking to you I tell you things I have never told anybody before—about my sister and the jellyfish, for instance. We have special and different kinds of conversations. In everyday life at home I have conversations about repairs to the car and the washing machine, and about the drains, the carpets, the flaking paint on the bannister, the rust marks on the ceiling.

Interviewer: Your house sounds like a wreck.

Virginia: I don't think it is, but when I compare my conversation with you with my conversation from day to day, I can see a huge difference.

Interviewer: Tell me about your house in New York then.

Virginia: Well, to begin with, it isn't in New York. The papers here have got that wrong; it's in Cambridge, Massachusetts. It is the house that used to belong to Gregory Pincus, one of the people who pioneered the contraceptive pill. When I moved in I searched for some memento, some relic of the historic former owner, but the house had been meticulously cleared out. Then one day I found a lone book behind a bookshelf and I was very pleased. It was *The Foxglove Saga*; have you read it? And by the way, if you want to get a different angle on some of this, you could talk to my sister Rosie. I have been away for so long and Rosie has been here all the time. I think you might find her quite interesting.

BOOK FOUR ·
THE RAMBLINGS OF
ROSIE O'DAY

*Cultures which essay to prevent incest between siblings often
manage to promote precisely the feelings they aim to inhibit,
thus making the prevention more difficult and yet more necessary, in a never-ending vicious circle—a kind of parody of
human good intentions.*

Robin Fox, *The Red Lamp of Incest*

Taking the suggestion of Virginia, Interviewer rang Rosie Quinlan (née O'Day) to ask for an interview and was invited to Greycliffe, the home of Rosie and Johara Quinlan and their family.
Greycliffe stands on the top of Magpie Hill in the rural outskirts
of Launceston. The walls of the house are made from bluestone
rubble which is two feet thick. Although built like a fortress,
the house is graceful and gabled; the surrounding countryside
can be seen for miles. Britton Jones, who built Greycliffe in 1836,
made sure that the house would be a lookout point. From there
he could watch for the approach of bushrangers or Aborigines.

Today the garden surrounding Greycliffe is planted with
old-fashioned roses and lavender hedges, as well as fruit trees,
a herb garden and a vegetable garden. The house is sheltered
from the winds by rows of pine trees. Rosie took Interviewer
walking in the grounds and across the fields close to the house.

Afterwards they had tea in the morning room which looks out across the rose garden. All the while Rosie talked.

'Virginia has come home after being away for nearly forty years. I remember her as someone who went off to the country to die when she was seventeen. She was starving herself to death, but something happened to her in Copperfield and she got better and then left to work in England and America. I remember her as a very self-centred person, and she hasn't changed. Because she is my sister I am pleased and interested to see her, and I am proud of the things she has done, but I don't really understand her. She did not come home when our parents died, but she has come home now to write a play for Nancy Best. As far as I can tell, Nancy Best and her brothers are rapidly turning the state into a sideshow. They own practically everything here, and now they have bought Virginia.

'I remember when the Bests started to buy up Trevallyn for the purpose of knocking it down to build the dome. I seem to be pretty much alone in my sentimental regret for the past which the Bests destroyed. What they have done is everywhere praised in the name of progress. But I am sad when I remember our old house, and the Quinlans' house nextdoor. And something that haunts me is the fact that when we sold the house we left my father's negatives in the cellar and now they have been buried forever. Doll wrote to me recently from Italy asking me to get certain negatives for her and I had to write back and tell her that the whole lot of them are buried under the Bluebird Café. "Would you be able," Doll wrote, "to send me the negatives of the pictures Dad took of me and the other prefects in the lab at school? I would love to show the others here the lab pictures because I have just been put in charge of the convent laboratory. We bottle the HMG here and send it all over the world for the IVF programmes. Imagine me!" Dear Doll, no, I can't imagine her. It was hard enough for me to envisage her as a nun in the first place, and then the order sent her to Italy, and now she's in a convent laboratory. My sisters have certainly turned out to be different from me.

'I am the middle girl. There was Virginia and Damien, and then me and Christopher and Doll. We lived next door to the Quinlans, and as things turned out I married Johara Quinlan and Damien married Philomena. Actually, what I remember most about the Quinlans in my childhood is the awful things we all did to FX. I was no exception. We used to make him eat slugs, and sometimes we would all sit on him. We hated him because he was not perfect, and we liked to think that we were. The only one who was decent to FX was Doll. She used to play with him for hours and teach him to do things and protect him from strangers.

'Once I was in the conservatory and I heard Doll and FX playing in the grass outside the window. At first I was scornful, but after a while I felt quite humble in the presence of Doll's patience and kindness. She was teaching him to add and sub-tract using clothes-pegs. And they had gardens. They turned the wilderness of our garden into a profusion of flowers and vegetables. They won prizes with their gladioli at the flower show, and FX bred a new pink gladi with a cream throat which he called Miss Doll O'Day. Later on, before the Quinlan's place was pulled down, FX had the most beautiful rose garden in Launceston. People felt sure, when the Bests bought the house they would keep the rose garden going.

'And they did, or FX did, for a while, but in the end every-thing had to go. It is strange to think that FX ended up as the boy Friday and right-hand man of The Best People. He was the only thing they kept when they got rid of everything. And the other thing I really think about a lot and find strange is the fact that what they built on the site of our old homes was the place, or the copy of the place, that Bedrock and Carrillo came from. I never went to Copperfield, and I never saw Bedrock and Car-rillo again after the time they came to stay with us, but they made a big impression on me, and I have somehow built on that impression over the years, and I have imagined often what

Copperfield must have been like. Because I had a version of Copperfield in my head, and because it was really quite special to me, I didn't want to go to the Museum Village. But I went one day with some friends who were visiting us from the mainland. It was nothing like what I had imagined and it made me sad. The worst place of all is the waxworks where they have got statues of Bedrock and Carrillo and Lovelygod. It seems very cruel to me. They even have a box where you can leave suggestions about how you think Lovelygod might have disappeared. We had a Japanese student staying with us for a while and she apparently became interested in the case of Lovelygod and did a whole history project on the topic. She took it back to Japan with her to be marked and so I never read it.

'Over the years Bedrock and Carrillo have become in my imagination like two great royal Egyptians from Ancient Egypt. Because they were twins and because they were lovers and because I always remember them as being so handsome and beautiful, I have thought of them as Ptolemy and Cleopatra. In the museum they look almost perfectly ordinary, except for their Titian hair. I never saw Lovelygod in real life, but in the display she is exactly like a doll. It seems that the history of Copperfield, the history of the Means, and of the mystery of Lovelygod, have had to become just part of the circus, part of the sideshow. I was actually quite surprised when our Japanese student decided to take it all so seriously and write her paper on it. It is as if the royal Means were too much for an ordinary society to cope with in the end, and they had to become statues alongside the native animals and the Aborigines and convicts.

'It is terrible to think that Bedrock spends her life in the ghost town of Copperfield mourning for her daughter and hoping for her return. The case which captured the public imagination to begin with because of the bizarre and colourful elements in it, gradually disappeared from view. I am inclined to think that it faded out *because* it became impossible for people to assimilate all the strange elements. There is even a school of thought that says Lovelygod never existed at all. The whole thing has become a curiosity, rather than the tragedy that it really is. Virginia's play on the subject will bring it all back into the limelight, but will also, I believe, remove it further into the realm of fairy-tale.

'There were people who said Bedrock and Carrillo had murdered Lovelygod, and other people who said old Philosopher had eaten her. Personally I imagine she must have walked in her sleep and fallen down a crack in the rock, been knocked unconscious, died, and was never discovered. Like the dog that virtually discovered the cave with the rock paintings in Altamira. He was able to bark so that his master could locate him and shift the stone that was blocking his way out of the cave. But if he couldn't make a noise ... I think that's what must have happened to Lovelygod.

'The public reaction completely split up Bedrock and Carrillo. I don't mean their relationship broke down in the ordinary way, but the result has been that Bedrock remains in the old Bluebird Café and Carrillo runs some centre for the finding of lost children in America. People tried to split them up before, of course. That's why they went to California in the first place, to get away from the taboos of the family and the town. I didn't think they would ever come back, but it seems they felt strongly sentimental about the press and the Palace, and when their parents could no longer run them, they took over. Do you know that the Bests even own the Bedrock Press now? And I meant to say that Bedrock and Carrillo had a secret language they worked out because they were twins. I often wonder whether they ever think in the secret language now they are apart. I believe they scarcely write to each other. My father always said their language sounded like Hungarian to him. And in fact, Carrillo published a Hungarian grammar at one stage. I should have a copy somewhere, as well as copies of some of his other books. I used to keep them with Virginia's books, but then one time I re-organized the bookshelves and I lost track.

'Did Virginia tell you she's going to write a book about

Launceston called *The Disappearance of the Public Library*? We
used to have such a dear old library. And speaking of things
like Carrillo's books—another thing I've got is one of the quilts
that Bedrock makes. Jack Fisher got it for me. He's marvellous
like that. In fact, I sometimes have thought that if it is possible
for anybody to know what happened to Lovelygod, Jack would
know.'

Rosie found Carrillo's Hungarian grammar and one of his
books about geology, and showed them to the visitor. She also
showed him the quilt that Bedrock had made using hundreds
of old floral scraps.

'I often think this quilt is rather like a book in itself,' Rosie
said. 'It even has a little piece of handkerchief in it that used to
belong to one of my teachers, Veronica World. It makes me sad
when I look at Bedrock's quilt, and I think of how she stays out
there in the bush sewing and thinking and hoping; and then I
look at what the Bests have made—I mean the Museum Village—and it reminds me of some vision by Hieronymus Bosch.
One of the worst things I saw when I went to the Museum
Village was the display of soul stones in a glass case. The Aborigines used to have special hollows in the ground where they
kept stones of a particular shape in a sort of nest. Like birds'
eggs. The place was secret and the stones were known as soul
stones because they stood for the secret power of their owner.
The owner would wash and brush the stones four times a year,
waiting until nobody was looking, taking the stones out of hiding, cleaning them, letting them dry in the sun, and then putting them back in the earth. The stones represented the secret
essence of their owner and they were magic objects on which
the life of the owner depended. When I saw the display of soul
stones in the glass case I cried.'

BOOK FIVE ·
WAITING FOR LOVELYGOD

And the daughter of the Pharoah came down to wash herself at the river; and her maidens walked along by the river's side; and when she saw the ark among the flags, she sent her maid to fetch it.

And when she had opened it she saw the child: and behold, the babe wept.

Exodus II: 5-6

In December 1989 the following article appeared in the *Los Angeles Times* under the heading 'Waiting for Lovelygod'.

Fireproof and earthquake resistant, the class-one steel and concrete of the foundations of the Great Mausoleum at Forest Lawn, Glendale, reach thirty-three feet into the bedrock of LA. The quiet Cathedral Drive that winds from the gates of the memorial park up to the Great Mausoleum passes the fountain and pool of 'The Finding of Moses'. The marble sculpture depicting the Pharoah's daughter finding the infant Moses in his cradle of bulrushes hidden in the flags by the riverside is a copy of a statue in the Pincio Gardens in Rome. It stands here in the pool at the entrance to the James Barrie Institute, the foundations of which also reach deep into the bedrock, defying earthquake and fire.

Dedicated to the search for lost children, the Institute is a symbol of hope. As the Great Mausoleum triumphantly defies death, so the James Barrie Institute denies the possibility of loss. All the windows look down on the statue of the Pharoah's daughter as she, a royal stranger, rescues the infant Moses from the stream. The wide, hushed corridors of the Institute are built from pale pink marble, and the technology which pulses and flashes throughout the edifice, sending and receiving messages of all types, storing and coding and classifying information twenty-four hours a day every day of the year, is invisible to the visitor. Over three million photographs of missing children hang in gold frames in the vast Hall of Reference.

Following the recent disappearance of two small children from Disneyland in broad daylight, I approached the Director of the Institute, Carrillo Mean, himself the father of a lost child, for an interview. I got much more than I bargained for from this interview, as it set me off on a journey of investigation to the other side of the globe.

On 17 August 1970, Lovelygod Mean disappeared overnight from her home in Copperfield, Tasmania, an island off the southernmost tip of the Australian continent. Recently in Copperfield I was able to visit and talk to Lovelygod's mother who keeps lonely vigil in the café of a ghost town. The café is the only habitable building in Copperfield nowadays, the surrounding shops and houses having fallen into decay in the years since the copper mine closed down.

I spoke also to a neighbouring farmer, Jack Fisher, who has lived in the area since he was born, and who explained how it was possible Lovelygod had been

virtually swallowed up by the forest which grows hor-
izontally and has been known to devour sheep, horses
and bushwalkers. Jack Fisher supplied two of the ac-
companying photographs which come from the collection of a Dr Vincent O'Day. These pictures demon-
strate the way of life in old rural Tasmania when
Copperfield was in its heyday. In the foreground of
the picnic photograph is F. X. Quinlan as a child. FX
was my guide and mentor in much of my investigative
journey. The other picture which recalls pictures of
the Russian royal family before Ekaterinburg, shows
members of Vincent O'Day's family with Lovelygod's
parents when they were very young. With F.X. Quinlan I spent many days in a new Tasmanian theme park
which particularly interested me, because it is a facsimile of the former town of Copperfield where the
child disappeared.

The theme park is on a hill overlooking a river
which moves at this point with great turbulence. Caves
in the rock face below the theme park were the sacred
meeting places of the extinct race of Aborigines that
used to inhabit the area. Escaped criminals from the
days of the early settlement by the English have also
left their mark on the landscape in the form of rocky
cairns used as places of lookout. An unusual feature
of the park is the glass dome in which it is sheltered.

On my second night in the town I went to a play
in the Gaiety Theatre of the theme park. The Gaiety
is a tiny Edwardian gem of a theatre where the columns holding up the dress circle are twisted like barley sugar and gilded like a Spanish Mission. Golden
ropes of silk hold back the velvet curtains of richest
claret that hang in the boxes. Cherubs drift across the
vaulted ceiling from which hang huge and brilliant
chandeliers. The curtain is claret velvet embossed

with gold and silver waratahs, the flowers which are the emblem of Tasmania. Being inside this theatre, which is an exact replica (constructed in modern materials which will stand the test of time) of the ghost-town theatre, was like being inside a jewel case. The boxes and the dress circle were filled with a crowd of politicians and local dignitaries in full regalia. An interesting point to note is that the most successful politicians here are named for colours—Gray, Brown, Green, Black and White—these names seem to assure a career in politics.

The play I saw was, by some coincidence, on the theme of Lovelygod Mean, the girl whose disappearance it was that brought me to Tasmania. The writer is one of the daughters of the aforementioned Vincent O'Day. Virginia O'Day is based nowadays in Cambridge, Mass., and has returned to her hometown only to write this play for the gala opening of the Gaiety. *Waiting For Lovely god* is in six scenes, each scene proposing a different solution to the disappearance. The audience makes up its own mind as to which version is the true one. The most dazzling theatre takes place in the scene where the girl ends up in a Russian circus. The part of Lovelygod is played throughout by a very talented local girl, Natasha Quinlan, and her acrobatic skill in the circus sequence is breathtaking.

The most chilling scene, for me, was the one where the child is taken by scientists for experiment. The interest that Lovelygod would have presented to the scientific world is not to be denied—she was the product of an old Tasmanian rural family in whose veins ran the blood of the extinct Aborigines as well as the blood of the English Means, who are descended from the de Means, who landed in England with William the Conqueror; her parents were close relatives of

each other; she suffered from the syndrome of primordial dwarfism.

In the ghost town I visited the local graveyard,
where I found the tombstones of Lovelygod's grandparents and great-grandparents. Her great-grandfa-
ther, Philosopher Mean, was a real local identity, a
character who kept a vast library out there in the wilderness and headed a small religious sect.

His temple is in fact reproduced in the theme park,
and is one of the most charming structures of its kind
I have seen. It is in the form of a small pyramid and
decorated with images and texts from all world religions. On the day of my visit, two weddings took place
at the temple; one couple was from the local Chinese
community which goes back hundreds of years in
these parts, and the other couple was Japanese, having flown in from their home country the day prior.

The brains behind this development in Tasmania
belong to a company called, appropriately, The Best
People. I met Nancy Best, the doyenne of The Best
People in her penthouse above the Casino, where I
was entertained in royal style. She is a self-made woman who makes no secret of the fact, having started out
in business peddling remedies from a wheelbarrow in
the streets of Launceston.

I am no closer to the truth of the whereabouts of
Lovelygod Mean than I was on the day I first visited
the James Barrie Institute in search of information on
the case which has come to be known as the Mickey
Mouse Mystery. But I sense that the spirit of Lovelygod has taken me on a real magic-carpet trip to the
other end of the earth, where the forest eats the horses
and life is in the hands of The Best People.

BOOK SIX ·
THE LAST NARRATOR

Let the reader reflect on the difficulty of looking at whole class-
es of facts from a new point of view.

Charles Darwin, *The Variation in Animals and Plants Under*
Domestication

Violets are red
Roses are blue
Sugar is sugar
And so are you.

F. X. Quinlan

Name:	Hanako Nakamo
Subject:	History
Mode:	Historical fantasy
Audience:	General
Topic:	The mysterious disappearance of Lovelygod Mean from her home in Copperfield, Tasmania on 17 August 1970

Research:	Newspaper files
	Interviews with local residents
	Photographs and documents held in the Historic Museum Village of Copperfield in Launceston
Inspiration:	Waxwork figure of Lovelygod Mean in the Waxwork Museum
	'The Birthday of the Infanta' by Oscar Wilde
	Freaks—Myths and Images of the Secret Self by Leslie Fiedler

A. Background information on myself and on why I undertook this particular project

In 1989 I spent three months as a Japanese exchange student in Tasmania, which is a large island off the south-eastern coast of Australia. I went to school at a state high school in the town of Kings Meadows where I made many good friends. At school I wore a blue skirt and blazer and a white shirt like an English schoolgirl.

My host family had the name of Quinlan which is an Irish name. I enjoyed very much my time with them in their house called Greycliffe. This is a stone house which was built last century on the top of a hill where it stands alone surrounded by a lovely garden and some pine trees. It commands an uninterrupted view of green fields and forests and rivers. Farms and some houses can be seen in the distance.

There are two children in the Quinlan family, Thomas and Rachel, and they have two dogs, a cat, a horse and sixteen bantams. Mr Quinlan is a dispensing pharmacist and he owns four shops. This is a tradition in his family. Mrs Quinlan is very busy looking after the family and the house. She is a very good cook and I was able to sample many traditional Australian dishes. I learned how to make pineapple upside-down cake, gravy, and

Yorkshire pudding. Every night we had dinner at Greycliffe and then we did our homework and watched television. We did not have to do very much homework.

On two occasions I went with my class to visit the Historic Museum Village of Copperfield. This is the facsimile of an old mining town and is also a tourist facility with a casino and a fun fair and a theme park. It is noteworthy because of the glass dome in which it is encased. I believe this to be the largest dome in the southern hemisphere, and the only dome in the world to contain a theme park.

In my English Literature class I studied the works of Oscar Wilde and was intrigued by the story 'The Birthday of the Infanta'. As part of my research in connection with this story I consulted Leslie Fiedler's book *Freaks,* and I became interested in the distinction drawn between dwarfs and midgets, the term 'dwarf' being reserved for grotesque humans who are large in the head and short in the legs, whereas the term 'midget' describes little people who are perfectly proportioned and beautiful. Fiedler uses two of the characters in *The Old Curiosity Shop* by Charles Dickens to give a striking literary example of the two types, dwarf and midget. 'The "goblin-like" Quilp represents the Dwarf as wicked lecher and persecutor of women, and the "fairy-like" Little Nell the Midget as Elf-child.'

When I visited the Historic Museum Village for the first time I was startled to see the arresting wax figure of a girl who suffered from primordial dwarfism, being, therefore a midget. The condition of primordial dwarfism is a rare one which produces perfectly proportioned miniature people who have always been popular in circuses and sought after by science.

B. The Essay

Lovelygod Mean was the great-great-granddaughter of one of the Tasmanian Aborigines who are now extinct. Lovelygod was born in Los Angeles in 1960 when her family was living in that city. They lived in the style known as 'hippie' or 'flower children', in a commune where the life was very free and where the use of hallucinatory drugs was common. The child failed to gain weight or to grow in the normal way, and yet she thrived and was a happy child, bright and very popular among the members of the commune. Her father sometimes obtained work as a violinist at Forest Lawn where musicians were required for funerals and weddings, and at the age of three Lovelygod began to perform ritual dances of great dignity at the Babyland section of the cemetery. She came to be much in demand for the funerals of young children. However, when she was five years old she and her parents returned to Tasmania to take over the responsibility of the family's hotel and printing press.

The town of Copperfield was in the remote north-western part of the island, and Lovelygod lived there in quiet seclusion for five happy years. She attended the local state school for a time and was a favourite with her classmates and teachers. She was treated, for the most part, as a normal child, although she was provided with small furniture and a seat in the front row. Her parents continued to consult specialists in the United States and in Switzerland where a large body of work has been completed on the syndrome. Doctors were unable to explain the child's condition or to offer any hope of therapy or change.

The Mean family were approached by theatrical agents with offers of a career for the diminutive child, but the family were firm in their statements that Lovelygod must finish her schooling before any decisions were taken.

When Lovelygod was ten years old, fate stepped in.

Imaginative Reconstruction of Events, Based on Available Evidence

In this account I will use the names of real people, but I must draw attention to the important fact that my essay is an historical fantasy.

On the spring night of 17 August, 1970, Lovelygod Mean retired to bed as was her custom at 8.30pm. She slept in a charming room which had once been a conservatory for flowers, at the
end of the verandah of the Palace Hotel. It was a quiet night at
the hotel in the mining town, and Lovelygod's mother, Bedrock
Mean, looked in on her sleeping daughter at approximately 11
pm when she went upstairs to bed.

'The clock on the stairs was chiming eleven when I turned
out the lights,' she said.

Silence fell upon Copperfield.

Three kilometres away in an open field a helicopter was
landing.

The pilot of the helicopter was F. X. Quinlan who had left
his car in Devonport and flown out to Copperfield. FX was the
son of a Launceston pharmacist, born in 1947. He grew up in the
leafy suburb of Trevallyn above the Cataract Gorge, in a large
and gracious home. His brothers and sisters married and moved
to other parts of the world, but FX remained at home with his
parents. When first his father and then his mother died in 1968,
the house was sold. It was acquired by Nancy Best who took
FX into her employ. He worked as a butler, chauffeur, guide
and pilot for the company named The Best People, continuing
to occupy his old family home, and showing great loyalty and
devotion to his employers. Nancy Best herself, resided in the
house next door.

The Best People have made a significant contribution to the
life and prosperity of Tasmania with their interest in many as-
pects of the entertainment, communications, and tourist indus-
tries. In 1987 when the time came for the Historic Museum Village of Copperfield to be constructed, The Best People erased
all the buildings of Trevallyn, locating three churches from the
area in a new religious settlement near the airport, and levelled
the land. But in 1970, FX and The Best People, and hundreds of
other families inhabited the graceful, old houses on the hill. It
was a peaceful, undisturbed existence. At this time, Nancy Best

spoke to her brother Bill.

'I wish we could persuade those people to let us take Lovelygod.'

FX overheard these words and he said to himself, 'I will make the wish come true.'

On 17 August when the moon sailed heedlessly in the dome of heaven, FX landed the helicopter in the lonely field and made his solitary way to the Palace. The clear, dark sky was sprinkled with bright stars. FX whistled to himself as he strode through the Back Woods, a fisherman's canvas bag slung across his back. His mind was concentrated on the one thought of bringing the child home with him, and he carried in his pocket a snapshot of Lovelygod that he had found in Nancy's office. He would carry this picture with him ever after; he would think of Lovelygod in future as 'my little girl'.

In the main street of Copperfield, FX's reflection slid across the windows. Soft as a moth FX padded along the verandah of the Palace. He pushed open the glass door and saw the child stir in her sleep as the cool night air touched her cheek. Fate, the moon, the planets, the gods, the time—all were on his side. For a few moments he stood looking down on the sleeping child. She was like a doll, and more beautiful than her picture would suggest. She was wax; she was peach; she was pearl; she was ivory. Lovelygod Mean was made from confectioner's sugar.

From his pocket, FX took the phial of chloroform and the cloth. In solemn ritual he sprinkled the drug onto the cloth, gazed once more at the sleeping face, and then placed the cloth firmly upon it. He slipped the limp and sleeping form, like a fish in a net, into the canvas bag. He left the door open in order to disperse the smell of chloroform, and then he made his way back through the woods to the field.

The people who lay sleeping in their beds in Copperfield were visited in dreams by the figure of a man in black bearing on his back a human burden. He mingled in their dreams with other visions of dream dread. The eyelids of the dreamers fluttered as the man travelled through the dreamers' minds. The bodies of the dreamers twitched in trouble, and the dreamers turned their heads back and forth on their dreaming pillows and fell into a deeper slumber, into a darker time.

A gate squeaked on its hinges in a faint, cold wind.

The sound made by the helicopter chopped its way into the dreams of sleeping farmers and their sleeping wives, potatoes, poppies, and wheat. Nobody woke.

FX left the helicopter in Devonport and drove his treasure to Trevallyn. Up the path to Nancy's house he carried the canvas bag in his arms like a cushion, a sacrifice, a dying child. He presented the bag to his employer with a wide and simple smile.

As white as snow, as clear as crystal, as clean as a whistle, as right as rain, as still as death, and as dead as a maggot. Like a fish out of water Lovelygod had died in the fishing bag from suffocation. A bag of game: a rabbit, a fox, a pheasant, a small kangaroo.

When Nancy Best saw and understood what had happened, what FX had done, she was white with rage.

'FX,' she said, 'you are an idiot.'

The body of the child was placed in the cellar of the house and the next day it was buried there without ceremony. In the world outside the cellar, circuses and scientists would never pause to gaze in delight and wonder at the diminutive figure of Lovelygod Mean. Police, newspapers, radio, television combed the forest, swept the skies, and dragged the seas and rivers. Fate and the gods had worked with F. X. Quinlan to leave no clues at all. The world came to Copperfield to search the eyes and hearts and depths of mother, father, teacher, preacher, friend and foe. The Best People were the vanguard of the search for Lovelygod Mean, offering a large reward for information.

The years passed and lost Lovelygod became a legend. F. X. Quinlan carried her picture with him always, sometimes taking it out of his pocket to show it to strangers.

'My little girl,' he explained.

Above the place where the child lay buried in the cellar grew the theme park of Copperfield. The unknown grave was marked by a café. If you can imagine the bustle and busy life that moved ceaselessly above the buried cellar; if you can imagine the bright blue bird shining on the roof, you can imagine the Bluebird Café.

A READER'S GUIDE TO THE BLUEBIRD CAFÉ

There is not perhaps a greater pleasure than an epistolatory communication between distant friends, and next perhaps to that, in intellectual enjoyment, is the dissemination of useful and entertaining information by means of the noble art of printing.

Henry Savery, *The Hermit in Van Diemen's Land*

ABIJAH

Son of Jeroboam, king of Israel. The story is told in the Old Testament book of Kings of how Abijah died in childhood because of his father's sins, according to the words of the prophet, Ahijah: 'And Jeroboam's wife arose, and departed, and came to Tirzah: and when she came to the threshold of the door, the child died.' I Kings 14:17.

A FIRST HUNGARIAN FOR TASMANIANS

Written by Carrillo Mean, *A First Hungarian*, to give it its popular title, was first published by the Bedrock Press (q.v.) in 1970, and has been a textbook in Tasmanian schools since that time.

AUGUST 17

The date on which Lovelygod Mean disappeared from her home, leaving no trace, in 1970. Also the date on which Azaria (q.v.) Chamberlain disappeared from the camping ground at Ayers Rock in Central Australia, in 1980.

ASHBY, LAVENDER CHRISTMAS

The first child to be enrolled at the Trafalgar (q.v.) school in Victoria in 1882.

AZARIA

A name meaning 'blessed of God'. The most common form of the name is *Uzziah,* although *Azariah* is occasionally seen.

Uzziah was one of the kings of Judah. He was the son of Jecholiah who was the wife of Amaziah, King of Judah. Amaziah was infamous for setting up idols for his gods. His son, Uzziah, prospered as long as he sought the Lord (II Kings 15:2) and did that which was right in the sight of the Lord. He developed the agriculture of Judah and also raised a large army. But he ultimately violated the priestly code and was stricken with leprosy.

BARRIE, SIR JAMES MATTHEW (1860-1937)

Author of the plays *Quality Street* and *The Admirable Crichton,* Barrie is best known as the author of *Peter Pan,* a play about a boy who never grew up. The play was written from stories Barrie made up for the sons of his friends Arthur and Sylvia Llewelyn Davies. The boys invented for him the name of Friendy-Wendy, and it was from this name that Barrie took the name of 'Wendy' in *Peter Pan.* The character of Peter is accompanied by a tribe of 'Lost Boys' who are babies who fell out of their prams and ended up in Neverland.

BECKETT, SAMUEL BARCLAY (1906-89)

Samuel Beckett was born at Foxrock near Dublin, educated at Trinity College, and went to Paris to teach English. He first reached a wide audience with the performance of *En Attendant Godot* in 1953.

BEDROCK

noun: 1. Geology: the solid rock under the soil and subsoil; 2. the bottom or lowest level of anything; 3. any firm or solid base.

BEDROCK PRESS

A press established in the 1930s in northern Tasmania by Philosopher Mean. Originally set up to publish works of philosophy and the history of religious thought, the press has become better known over the years for such titles as *The Tried and Tested* (q.v.), *A First Hungarian For Tasmanians, Igneous Intrusions in Southern Tasmania, The Lost Child in the Australian Psyche, The Meaning of Mining, Trekking Tasmania* and *The Mining of Meaning* by Carrillo Mean.

BEES

Bees were introduced to the colony of Van Diemen's Land in 1821. The event was reported in the *Hobart Town Gazette* of 27 April that year: 'A hive of bees in the best possible state of health and condition has been brought out by the ship *Mary* from Liverpool, and has been presented by Mr Kermode, owner of that vessel, to the Lieutenant-Governor. The bee has not before been imported into Van Diemen's Land.'

Swarms from these and other imported hives escaped into

the bush, and rapidly increased in numbers.

BEST, BILL, NANCY AND OLIVER

Descendents of John Best, convicted at the Old Baily in 1783 of theft of goods valued at thirty-nine shillings, and sentenced to seven years' transportation. Best, with a group of other convicts, mutinied on board the ship which was taking them to America. He stood trial again and was sent to Norfolk Island in 1788. He ended his days as a small landowner in Penrith, South Australia.

A more modern English relative of Bill, Nancy and Oliver Best was George Best who, in 1926, discovered Agatha Christie's abandoned car on the morning after the writer's disappearance. George Best, the well-known English soccer player, is another distant relative.

BLUEBIRD

1. In popular imagination a bright blue bird in the form of a swallow (q.v.) signifying hope and happiness; 2. the name given by Sir Malcolm Campbell (1885-1948), the British racing motorist who set world speed records on land and water, to all his racing cars and boats. It was the name of the speedboat in which Sir Malcolm Campbell's son, Donald, was killed when attempting to break his own world record in 1967. The speed (328 mph) at which he crashed is still the unofficial world record; 3. a North American thrush of the genus *Sialia* with much blue in the plumage of the male. There are three species, and the Eastern Bluebird (*Sialia sialis*) which inhabits the eastern part of the continent has endeared itself to people by its early spring arrival, by the pretty notes of its plaintive song, and by its gentle appearance and bright blue plumage. The Western Bluebird (*Sialia mexicana occidentalis*) is of a deeper blue than the Eastern Bluebird. And the Mountain Bluebird has a pale blue breast and is a remarkably silent bird.

'BLUE BIRD OF HAPPINESS'

A popular melody written by Sandor Harmati, with words by
Edward Heyman.

BLUE BIRD, THE

A play written in 1908 by the Belgian dramatist, essayist and
philosopher Maurice Maeterlinck (1862-1949). In this poetic
fantasy, sister and brother Mytyl and Tyltyl, search for the Blue
Bird which will bring happiness. Even the stage directions read
like fairy tale:

*The key has hardly touched the door before its tall and wide
leaves open in the middle, glide apart and disappear on either side in
the thickness of the walls, suddenly revealing the most unexpected
of gardens, unreal, infinite and ineffable, a dream-garden bathed in
nocturnal light, where, among stars and planets, illumining all they
touch, flying ceaselessly from jewel to jewel and from moonbeam to
moonbeam, fairy-like blue birds hover perpetually and harmonious-
ly down the confines of the horizon, birds innumerable to the point
of appearing to be the breath, the azured atmosphere, the very sub-
stance of the wonderful garden.*

BP

Initials signifying The Best People and also British Petroleum.

BRADY, MATTHEW (1799-1826)

Sentenced in 1820 at the Salford Assizes for stealing a basket
of bacon, butter and rice. The sentence was for seven years in
Van Diemen's Land. In June 1824 he escaped in a whaleboat
with thirteen other prisoners. They went ashore on the Der-
went River and robbed a homestead of guns and provisions and
began to live in the bush. They formed the Brady Gang, Mat-

thew Brady becoming a popular hero throughout the island. Matthew Brady was captured by John Batman and sentenced to be hanged. When he was waiting for his execution, his cell was filled every day with visitors bringing baskets of flowers and fruit and cakes.

BRENDAN THE NAVIGATOR, St (486?—575?)

Probably born near Tralee. Very few details of his life can be asserted with certainty. His most important monastic foundation was Clonfert. Like many other Irish monks of the period he was a great traveller, and his cult owes much to the visionary fairy-story 'The Navigation of St Brendan', which transforms the historical, seafaring abbot into a mythical adventurer who, with sixty companions in skin-covered coracles set off to discover the Isles of the Blessed, travelling for seven years with a floating monastery, and reaching the Canaries and Greenland.

Brendan's rule of life is said to have been dictated to him by an angel. He foresaw that at his death attempts would be made by the faithful to claim his body. So he directed that his death should be kept secret while his remains were taken to the abbey at Clonfert in a cart, disguised as his own luggage.

The feast of St Brendan is on 16 May.

CHERRY RIPE SLICES

6½ oz butter, ½ cup sugar, 2 tablespoons cocoa, 1 egg, beaten, ½ cup chopped walnuts, ½ cup coconut, 8 oz Marie biscuits

For the filling

2 oz chopped glacé cherries (red), 3 oz melted copha, 1 tablespoon castor sugar, 2-3 drops cochineal, 8 oz coconut, ½ tin condensed milk

For the topping

3 oz cooking chocolate, 1 oz butter

To make the base

Melt butter, add sugar and cocoa and bring to the boil. Add egg, beat well, cook one minute. Pour over walnuts and coconut and crushed biscuits. Stir well and press into greased tin.

To make the filling

Combine all ingredients and press onto the base.

To make the topping

Chop chocolate roughly and place in a metal bowl over hot water. Add butter and stir until blended. Spread over filling. Allow to cool. Chill. Cut into squares.

COCKROACH

Known as the black beetle, although its colour is really brown, the cockroach cannot claim any very close affinity to the hard-shelled beetle tribe. Cockroaches are members of the straight-winged (*Orthoptera*) order of insects. They are much flattened from above and below, which enables them to hide in crevices during the day, and the upper pair of wings is merely leathery, instead of being horny as in beetles. In the female of the common cockroach the wings do not develop, and are represented by mere scales, and those of the male cover only half of the body. The front part of the fore-body is developed into a broad shield under which the insect hides its head. The mouth is furnished with powerful jaws. There is a pair of very long, flexible antennae, and the long legs are covered with strong bristles.

A nocturnal insect. A house that swarms with cockroaches might appear in the daytime to be free of them, but for the unpleasant odour characteristic of them. The eggs are contained in little horny purses, which are deposited in crannies. Each purse contains 16 eggs. The common cockroach is an alien that came from the East. There are three native species, quite small creatures which never come into houses, but the alien, used to warmer conditions, only ventures out of doors in the hottest weather for the purpose of establishing itself in neighbouring houses. There is a smaller and paler species known as the Croton bug (*Blatella germanica*) which emanates from Central Europe.

A good remedy against the cockroach is to strew its nocturnal haunts with fresh slices of cucumber, which, being consumed render the cockroaches helpless. Beetle traps which entice them to fall into beer and get drowned may also be used with success in reducing numbers. A more deadly device is spreading phosphor paste on thin bread or mixing it with honey. Arsenic added to potato boiled or mashed, or mixed with the pulp of a roasted apple, is a certain remedy.

COPPERFIELD

A small town on the Welcome River in the far north-west of Tasmania. Copper was discovered in the area by Philosopher Smith (q.v.) and when production of the ore was at its peak in the 1930s, the town of Copperfield was a lively centre of industry and culture. In 1970 the mine was closed, and since that time the town has all but disappeared. Some attempts have been made to re-open the mine, but these have been unsuccessful. Copperfield is best known outside Tasmania as the location of the celebrated disappearance of a child on 17 August 1970. The case remains unsolved. Copperfield has been reproduced in facsimile at a theme park in Launceston.

DALRYMPLE, 'DOLLY' (1812-64)

One of the first Tasmanian children to have a native Tasmanian mother and a European father.

Her father, George Briggs, came to Australia in 1806 when he was fifteen. He worked as a sealer in Bass Strait, and as a result came to know the Trawlwoolway people of Cape Portland in the north-east of Tasmania. The chief of the Trewlwoolway treated George Briggs almost as one of his own people, and offered him his daughter Worrete-moete-yenner as his wife. The couple had two daughters, Dolly being the second one.

The Trawlwoolway people hated the children born to women of the tribe by white men, and frequently killed them. One evening at sunset, Worrete-moete-yenner sat with her first daughter and other members of the tribe beside a fire in the bush. Without warning, the child was snatched from her arms and thrown into the fire. The baby was treated by a white doctor, but died a few days afterward.

Dolly was born in 1812, and before she was two years old, she was given to foster parents, Dr Jacob Mountgarret and his wife, Bridget. She was given the name of Dalrymple (q.v.) Mountgarret Briggs, known as Dolly, and was taught to read and write and sew.

When Dolly was fourteen she left the Mountgarrets and went to live with Thomas Johnson who was not free to marry because he was an assigned convict. She was accepted by neither the Aborigines nor by the white settlers. Dolly defended her home and her children against a group of Aborigines who tried to set fire to the house. As a result of her courage, Dolly was granted twenty acres of land in Perth, and permission to marry Thomas Johnson. They had thirteen children. Worrete-moete-yenner was given permission by the Governor to live with Dolly and her family. The family moved to Latrobe where they acquired large areas of land, built the house Sherwood Hall, bought two hotels, and a hall for church services, public meetings, and for a school. They cleared the trees on their land and split the wood into palings which were sent to Victoria and South Australia. And they opened the Alfred Colliery in 1855. Dolly Dalrymple died on 1 December 1864.

DALRYMPLE, PORT

The name given by Matthew Flinders to the place which was to become Launceston. The name 'Dalrymple' was chosen in honour of Alexander Dalrymple who was an hydrographer with the East India company, and a fierce critic of the export of British prisoners to the Australian colonies. Dalrymple was of the opinion that felons would see transportation to the colonies as an inducement to commit crimes.

DARWIN, CHARLES ROBERT (1809–82)

Charles Darwin is best known for his argument for a natural, rather than a divine, origin for the human race. He was born in Shrewsbury and in 1831 he went to South America on the *Beagle*, returning to England in 1836 to publish, in 1839, the *Journal of Researches into the Geology and Natural History of the various countries visited by H.M.S. Beagle*. In 1859 his greatest work, *On the Origin of Species by Means of Natural Selection,* was published. He published *The Descent of Man* in 1871. Charles Darwin visited Australia briefly during the voyage of the *Beagle*.

'No fact in the long history of the world is so startling as the wide and repeated extermination of its inhabitants.' C. R. Darwin

DICKENS, CHARLES JOHN HUFFHAM (1812–70)

The happiest period of the early childhood of Charles Dickens was followed by a time of intense misery when his father was imprisoned for debt, and Charles, at the age of twelve, was sent to work in a factory where he pasted the labels on blacking bottles. Memories of this time inspired much of his fiction, notably the early chapters of *David Copperfield*. He married Catherine Hogarth and they had a large family. He and Catherine separated in 1858 when he fell in love with Ellen Ternan, a young actress. At this time Dickens gave many energetic readings of his work. He died suddenly, leaving his novel *The Mystery of Edwin Drood* unfinished.

DOLL

A pet form of the name Dolores (Sorrow) and Dorothea (Gift of God). The most common meaning of the word 'doll' is 'a toy which resembles a person', and the most common type of doll is a miniature girl-child. When applied to women, the term 'doll' is derogatory, having a similar meaning to 'moll', meaning 'harlot, slattern, slut'. A 'badly dressed maid-servant' is known as a 'dolly', as is the smallest pig in a litter.

EKATERINBURG

The city in the Soviet Union where, in 1918, Czar Nicholas II and his family were executed. In 1924 the name of the city was changed to Sverdlovsk. It is a major industrial and cultural centre.

EXTINCT

By the definition of the World Wild Life Fund of Australia, a species of animal life is deemed to be officially non-existent when a period of fifty years has elapsed since the last officially confirmed sighting of a member of the species. According to this definition, the thylacine (q.v.) has been extinct since September 1986. Other Australian animals recently declared extinct include the desert rat-kangaroo, the hare-wallaby, the pig-footed bandicoot, the crescent nail-tailed wallaby, and the toolache wallaby. According to the Australian Museum in Sydney, a species of animal (or plant) life now becomes extinct every six hours.

EYE OF GOD

In the thought of ancient Egypt, the eye is the commonest symbol. It was always the symbol of the Great Goddess. The two eyes were considered to be separate, one being the sun and one the moon. The Egyptian image of the Eye of God is of a falcon's eye, referring to the fact that the first High God of the Egyptians was a falcon. The eye represents omniscience and the faculty of intuitive vision. It also depicts the androgyne as being formed of the oval female symbol and the circle of the male. A triangle with the Eye as the centre is a reminder of the all-seeing Eye of God. Egyptian literature abounds in allusions to 'bringing back the Eye', referring to the motif of the return of the conquering hero.

FIRETAIL

Known as the Beautiful Firetail (*Enblema bella*), the Firetail is a small bird (six inches long) found in south-eastern Australia. It lives in scrub country, heath country, and in forest gullies. It is a shy bird and feeds on seeds and insects. The sexes are similar in their plumage, being dark grey above, grey below, and striped all over with fine blackish brown lines. The bill and rump are of startling bright crimson.

FISHER, JACK

Back Woods farmer, son of King and Queenie Fisher. The Fishers of the Back Woods are descendants of James Cowley Morgan Fisher who was known as the Forest Hill Messiah. In 1868,

James Fisher and his followers, who were known as The Fisher-
ites, built a temple in Forest Hill, Victoria. The Fisherite sect
has been compared to the Christian Israelites, and it combined
elements of faith from many different religions.

GINGER BEER 'PLANT'

Put into an airtight bottle 8 sultanas, juice of 2 lemons, a teaspoon of lemon pulp, 4 teaspoons sugar, 2 teaspoons ground
ginger, and 2 cups cold water. Let ferment 3 days. Then daily for
a week, add 2 teaspoons ginger and 4 teaspoons sugar. To make
the ginger beer, put 4 cups of boiling water, juice of 4 lemons,
and 4 cups of sugar in a large container and strain the 'plant'
contents (through muslin) into it, squeezing dry. Add 28 cups
cold water, bottle and seal. Makes about 12 bottles, which will
be ready for use in 5 days. Halve the squeezed 'plant' and put in
a jar with 2 cups of water. Feed each week for 2 weeks teaspoons
ginger and 4 teaspoons sugar.

GOETHE, JOHANN WOLFGANG VON (1749–1832)

For many years Goethe was the director of the Weimar court
theatre. His most celebrated work is the poetic drama *Faust*.

GREENE, (HENRY) GRAHAM (1904–)

Graham Greene, novelist and playwright, was educated at
Berkhamsted school where his father was the headmaster. His
range as a writer is wide, and his preoccupations include moral
dilemma, good and evil, and life in a world which has come
to be known as 'Greeneland' and which is characterized by its
seediness. Graham Greene has said that if he were to choose an
epigraph for his novels he would quote from *Bishop Blougram's
Apology*:

Our interest's on the dangerous edge of things,
The honest thief, the tender murderer,
The superstitious atheist ...

HANAKO

A Japanese girl's name meaning 'Flower Child'.

HEAVENLY TART

Coconut Jelly

1 cup water, juice two lemons, ½ cup sugar, 1 tablespoon arrow-root, cochineal

Blancmange

1 cup milk, 1 tablespoon cornflour, 1 tablespoon butter, 2 table-spoons castor sugar

To make the jelly, boil water together with lemon juice and sugar, add arrowroot mixed in a little extra water, stir over heat till thickened, add few drops cochineal, cool slightly and pour into pastry shell to set.

To make the blancmange, heat milk and add cornflour mixed with a little extra milk. Stir over heat until thickened, add butter and sugar and mix well. Cool slightly then pour gently onto jelly layer. Sprinkle top with coconut.

HMG

Human Menopausal Gonadotrophin: a hormone administered to women in the process known as 'the treatment of infertility'. Australian doctors obtain the hormone from European convents where the urine of suitable nuns is collected in specially designed stainless steel vessels. Supplies in Australia may be obtained from the chemical company Organon, or from the Commonwealth Serum Laboratories.

HMV

Initials signifying the Historic Museum Village and also the recording label His Master's Voice.

HOSPITALITY MERINGUE PIE

Ingredients

2 cups dried apricots

2 cups cold water

1 tablespoon each cornflour and butter, sugar, short-crust

2 egg yolks, egg-whites

sugar for meringue

Soak the apricots overnight in the cold water. Cook gently till soft, rub through sieve, replace in saucepan. Moisten cornflour with cold water. Add butter, moistened cornflour and sugar to taste to apricot purée and cook till thickened, then allow to cool. Line a pie-dish with short-crust and bake. Beat the 2 egg yolks thoroughly and add to the cool apricot mixture. Pour into a pie-dish. Cover with meringue and brown in a moderate oven.

ISIS (GODDESS)

Isis was the daughter of the Egyptian sky goddess, Nut, who was the wife of the sun god Ra. Nut gave birth to Osiris, Horus, Set, Nephtys and Isis. Set married his sister Nephtys; and Osiris married his sister Isis. Osiris was wise and popular, and his brother, Set, was jealous of him, and joined with seventy-two conspirators to plot against Osiris. Set fashioned a beautiful box into which Osiris would fit exactly. Then he and the seventy-two conspirators invited Osiris to a banquet. During the feasting Set said he would give the box to any person who fitted into it. The last person to try the box was Osiris who of course fitted it exactly. As soon as Osiris was in the box, the conspirators closed the lid on him and soldered it down with molten lead. Then they flung the box into the waters of the Nile.

When Isis heard of the fate of Osiris she cut off a lock of her hair, put on mourning attire, and wandered up and down beside the river seeking the body of her husband and brother. The coffer containing the body of Osiris at last drifted ashore at Byblus on the Syrian coast. In the place where the coffer landed a tamarisk tree was growing, and this tree reached out and embraced the coffer so that the body of Osiris became enclosed in the tamarisk's trunk. The king of the land, admiring the tree for its beauty, had it cut down and fashioned into a pillar for his palace. When Isis learned of this, she journeyed to Byblus and sat down by the well, her face wet with tears. The handmaidens of the king came to her and Isis greeted them kindly. She braided their hair and breathed on them so that a wondrous perfume from her divine body surrounded them. They took her to the palace where Isis, now in the likeness of a swallow (q.v.), fluttered round the pillar that contained the body of Osiris, twittering mournfully. Isis finally revealed herself to the king and she begged for the pillar to be given to her. The king gave the pillar to Isis, and she at once fell upon it and embraced it, and lamented. Her cries were so vehement that one of the children of the king died of fright. Isis put the coffer in a boat and sailed away.

The wicked brother, Set, overtook Isis and he rent the body of Osiris in fourteen pieces which he scattered in the water. Isis now sailed up and down the marshes in a shallop made from papyrus, searching for the pieces of her husband's body. She discovered every portion save the genital member of Osiris, for this part had been eaten by a crab. Isis re-assembled the body of Osiris, fashioning the missing member from a piece of cedar. With the resurrected body of her husband and brother, Isis conceived their son Horus.

ISIS (RIVER)

Small central Tasmanian river named after the English River Isis.

JOHARA, St (ll62?-I252?)

Feast day formerly I April was suppressed in the Roman Calendar of 1969 when the Holy See reduced the feast to the dimension of a merely local cult. There was at the time a sharp reaction in various countries, led in Italy by a committee of popular stars of the cinema. The feast has continued to be celebrated with growing rather than reduced fervour.

Johara was the son of a wealthy merchant with property and interests in the northern states of Germany. The exact date and place of the saint's birth are lost, but a story telling of a swarm of bees which entered the chamber at the time of birth, survives. The midwife was blinded by the stings of the bees and dropped the child who remained unharmed. Some hours later, tears from the child's eyes fell on the eyes of the midwife whose sight was immediately restored. The midwife retired to a remote hermitage and passed her life in fasting and prophecy, foretelling the fact that Johara would bring the word of God, sweet as honey, to many distant pagan peoples.

So pure was Johara in thought, word and deed that when confined to bed with a childhood illness, he begged for socks lest his naked feet should rub together in his feverish sleep.

When Johara was sixteen a horde of Visigoths overran his village. When the invaders approached the doors of the church with flaming brands, Johara fell to his knees in their path, and a company of bears, larger than any bears ever seen in the district, emerged from the forest and devoured the Visigoths.

Johara lived for ten years as a hermit, sleeping for two hours each night, rolling in brambles, keeping silence and existing on the juice of herbs.

He was invited to Paris and appointed Bishop of St Denis. Beneath his hands the lame walked, the blind saw, and the deaf could hear the sounds of birds and the chanting of the religious in the choir. One night a band of starving peasants came to his door and he had no food to give them. Seized by inspiration, Johara made the sign of the cross over his bath-water which changed into sweet mead. His fame spread.

He founded an order of women, the Little Sisters of the Divine Heart-throb, which is still active in the education of girls in Paris and in centres as remote as Cuzco and Flinders Island.

He retired to lead a life of prayer and penance in a hermitage in the grounds of the Heart-throb convent, and when he was nearly ninety years old, one of the sisters observed a dove rising in a cloud of gold from the roof of the hermitage. The body of the saint was discovered in the hermitage, seated at his rustic table, a sweet smile on his lips and an empty nest of pure gold cradled in his hands. Dispute arose whether Johara's holy body should be buried at the convent or at the cathedral. This dispute was settled when the body, before the astonished eyes of the quarrelling cardinals and nuns, divided and separated so that two bodies were present where there had been only one. It is not surprising that St Johara is a patron of scientists involved in the work of cloning human tissue. He is also the patron of hosiers.

LAURA POWER'S APPLE CAKE

Ingredients

4 Granny Smith apples, sugar to taste (preferably brown), 1½ cups self-raising flour, 2 teaspoons cinnamon, 5 oz butter, ½ cup castor sugar, 1 egg

Peel, cut up and stew apples and sweeten to taste. Set aside. Sift dry ingredients into a basin, rub in butter and add sugar. Bind together with beaten egg. A little milk may be added to make a pliable dough. Divide mixture in half and roll out until it is about ten inches square. Place on well-greased tray. Leave the edges of the dough rough. Spread cool, drained apples on the dough, half an inch from the edge. Roll out the remaining dough and place over the apples. Bake in a moderate oven for half an hour. When cool, the cake may be dusted with icing sugar and cut into slices (squares).

MEANING OF MEANING, THE

A study of the influence of language upon thought and of the science of symbolism, by C. K. Ogden and I. A. Richards. Published by Routledge & Kegan Paul.

NABOKOV, VLADIMIR VLADIMIROVIVICH (1899–1977)

A Russian novelist, poet, literary scholar and lepidopterist. He was born in St Petersburg, the eldest child of a liberal statesman. In 1919 the family left Russia to live in Germany. Nabokov studied in Cambridge, and also lived in Berlin. He went to the United States with his wife and son in 1940. By 1959 his novels were being written in English, whereas before that they had been written in Russian. When his novel *Lolita,* published in the United States in 1958, became an outstanding success, Nabokov was able to give up teaching and devote his time to writing. He taught at Wellesley College (1941–48) and at Cornell University (1948–59). When at Wellesley, he held a Harvard Research Fellowship in lepidoptery. He died in Switzerland where he had lived since 1959.

PARADISE

1.) A small country town in north-western Tasmania;

2.) In most traditions Paradise is an enclosed garden, a garden-island, or a Green Isle. It signifies a place of perfect harmony between God and Creation. It also represents the innermost soul and a place where time stands still. It is a place where heaven is so close to earth that it can be reached by climbing a tree, a vine or a mountain.

Paradise is an enclosed space surrounded by a barrier such as the sea, and is open only to the sky. The Tree of Life and the Tree of Knowledge stand at the centre of Paradise, and from the roots of the Tree of Life flows a fountain which gives rise to the four Rivers of Paradise.

Paradise is a place of bird song and scented flowers, and is commonly thought to be a rose garden. Paradise Lost plunges mankind into time and darkness; Paradise Regained restores unity and ends time.

PEACOCK, CATHERINE FAIRY

In the early 1920s Fairy Peacock, from the general store at Healesville in Victoria, drove a jinker around the orchards delivering the mail.

PHOENIX

In the language of Alchemy, the phoenix represents the *magnum opus.*

Wherever it is found it is a symbol of death and rebirth by fire, of resurrection and of immortality. The phoenix is a fabulous bird which dies by self-immolation. It remains dead for three days and then rises again from its own ashes. It is symbolic of the sun as it is the fire bird, signifying divine royalty, nobility and uniqueness. Also, it represents gentleness since it crushes nothing upon which it alights, and it feeds on no living thing, existing on dew.

In the Garden of Paradise, the phoenix is always associated with the rose.

It has the head of a cock and the back of a swallow, giving it attributes of the sun and the moon. Its wings are the wind, its tail represents trees and flowers, and its feet are the earth.

The appearance of a phoenix is highly auspicious and signifies peace, benevolent rule, or the appearance of a great sage.

ROCK CAKES

Rub 3 oz butter into 8 oz plain flour. Add 4 oz currants and sultanas, 3 oz sugar and a teaspoon of baking powder. Beat an egg and stir it into a gill of milk. Add this gradually to the mixture and stir thoroughly. Put in little rough heaps on a well-greased tray. Bake in a very hot oven for 10–15 minutes.

SAND CAKE

2 eggs, 4 oz butter, 4 oz sugar, 4 oz ground rice, 3 oz self-raising flour, ½ teaspoon vanilla

Cream butter and sugar. Add eggs one at a time, beating well. Sift in ground rice and beat well for five minutes. Sift in the flour and fold lightly. Bake in a well-greased square tin for one hour in a moderate oven. When cold, pour over soft icing and decorate with crystallized fruits and nuts.

SAVERY, HENRY (1791–1842)

The first Australian novelist and essayist. He was born in Somerset, the son of a Bristol banker. In 1819–22 he was the editor of the *Bristol Observer*. The partner in a sugar refining company, he forged bills to meet his debts. The forgery was discovered and Henry Savery was tried, found guilty, and condemned to death. He was, however, reprieved, and transported to Van Diemen's Land where he arrived in 1825. In prison in Hobart, he wrote about life in the colony. This writing was published in the *Colonial Times* and later, in 1830, was published as *The Hermit in Van Diemen's Land*, the first book of Australian essays.

Henry Savery's novel *Quintus Servinton,* published in 1831, was the first Australian novel.

Henry Savery obtained a conditional pardon in 1838, but was again convicted of forgery and was sent to the prison at Port Arthur where he died in 1842.

SCRIPTURE CAKE

½ lb. butter	Judges 5:25
1 cup sugar	Jeremiah 6:20
1 cup warm pumpkin	Psalms 63:5
1½ cups plain flour	1 Kings 4:22
1½ cups self-raising flour	1 Kings 4:22
3 eggs	Isaiah 10:14
2 cups figs	1 Samuel 30:12

2 cups raisins   1 Samuel 30:12

Pinch salt   Leviticus 2:13

Spices to taste   1 Kings 10:10

Follow Solomon's rule for making good boys (Proverbs 23:14) and you will have an excellent cake. Bake in moderate oven. (Sultanas can be substituted for figs.)

SMITH, JAMES ('PHILOSOPHER')

On 4 December 1871, Philosopher Smith discovered 'a mountain of tin' at Mount Bischoff, Tasmania, where one of the most important tin mines in the world would be established. He was the first person to explore the back country of West Devon from Cape Grim to Cradle Mountain, and discovered gold, silver and copper, as well as the beautiful pencil pine.

SWALLOW

noun: Long-winged, graceful, migrating bird which catches insects while flying. Swallows have forked tails and steel blue upper plumage. In many parts of the world they are welcomed as heralds of the spring, and the general belief is that they are birds of good omen.

Peking was known as the City of Swallows because of the custom of allowing the swallows to nest inside the houses where they were given a household shrine. Many peoples have believed that the swallow hibernated in mud during the winter and was revitalized in the spring. Hence the swallow is a symbol of rebirth and hope. It has always been known as a sacred bird, and as such is to be feared as well as respected. A swallow appearing in a dream is a portent of untimely death, as is a swallow flying down a chimney.

In Spanish legend, the swallow acquired the reddish patch on its breast when it attempted to peck out the thorns from Christ's crown. The swallow is one of the birds of the goddess Venus, and its shape is compared to the female pudendum. And the goddess Isis (q.v.) took the shape of a swallow and is sometimes invoked in this form.

The typical attitude to the swallow is one of ambivalence. It was a tradition in ancient Greece that a swallow entering the house is a bad omen. The women of the house caught the swallow, poured oil over it, and freed the house of evil by releasing the bird into the open air. In Sumatra there is a traditional belief that a childless woman will conceive if a sacrifice is made of three grasshoppers, and if a swallow is then set free. The curse of infertility will then fall upon the swallow and fly away with it;

verb: To take through the mouth and gullet to the stomach. Opinion is divided as to whether the noun and the verb share a common origin. Partridge in *Origins* puts forward the theory that the bird was so named from the verb because of the habit of flying with an open beak and catching insects and swallowing them in flight.

TAMAR

The childless widow of Er, and then of his brother, Onan, Tamar became the mother of twins by her father-in-law, Judah. (Genesis 38:6, 11, 13, 24)

TAMAR (RIVER)

A tidal river formed by the confluence of the North and South Esk rivers in northern Tasmania. The city of Launceston is situated at the head of the Tamar which flows into Bass Strait.

THYLACINE

Known as the Tasmanian Tiger, this animal is now registered as extinct (q.v.) by the World Wild Life Fund of Australia. The scientific name of the thylacine is *Thylacinus cynocephalus*. It is the only member of the poly-protodont marsupial family to exist in modern times, and is the largest carnivorous marsupial to have live in historical times.

A body of naturalists, zoologists and members of the general public believes that the thylacine, although officially unsighted for fifty years, has retreated to remote parts of Tasmania where it lives in secrecy. From time to time people claim to have caught sight of a thylacine, but no evidence acceptable to the Wild Life Fund has been presented in support of the case for the animal's existence.

The thylacine is a large animal with superficial resemblance to a wolf, having prominently striped hind quarters, the coat being the colour of sand. The jaws are long and powerful and contain 46 teeth. At the beginning of British settlement in Tasmania in 1803 the thylacine was widespread but did not exist in great numbers. It soon came to the notice of settlers as a killer of sheep and poultry, and the Van Diemen's Land Company which had extensive properties in the far north-west of the island offered a bounty for the carcases of thylacines, and employed as well a trapper. The government introduced a further bounty in 1888. Traders bought live thylacines for sale to zoos, and the animals were exhibited in England, Germany and America. People discovered that thylacines would not breed in captivity. In July 1936 the Tasmanian government declared the thylacine to be a 'fully protected animal', and the last captive thylacine died in the Hobart Zoo in September 1936. Since that time much effort has been given to the search for the thylacine by people using snares, box traps, and automatic cameras. Such evidence of the animal's existence as has been found has been inconclusive.

One of the finest portraits of a thylacine is to be seen on the labels of bottled beer. A team of Japanese designers and technicians recently constructed a facsimile of a thylacine which is indistinguishable from a living animal. And a computer, taking all available data, has offered proof that the thylacine is still in existence in some as yet undiscovered location in Tasmania.

TRAFALGAR

A town on the Princes Highway in Gippsland, Victoria.

TRAFALGAR, BATTLE OF

A naval battle in the Napoleonic Wars. This battle took place on 21 October 1805. The British fleet was victorious, defeating the French at Cape Trafalgar, which is between Cadiz and Gibraltar.

TRIED AND TESTED, THE

Collected recipes of women of Tasmania, first published in 1952 by the Bedrock Press. (Selected recipes can be found throughout this Guide.)

TRUGANINI (1812–76)

A member of the South-east tribe of Tasmanian Aborigines, Truganini was born the year before the city of Hobart was founded by British settlers. By 1830 the Governor of Tasmania (at that time known as Van Diemen's Land) was offering a bounty of five pounds for every adult Aborigine captured alive, and two pounds for every child. Truganini was one of a small group of Aborigines who, in spite of brutal treatment by many white people, attempted to cooperate with the government and to improve the lives of the Aborigines as well as the relations between black and white people.

Truganini's name was changed to Lallah Rooke, the name of a beautiful Indian princess. Truganini was a diminutive woman, being four feet three inches tall. She saw her people die out, and she saw scientists excavate the Aboriginal cemetery at Oyster Cove, digging up skulls. Truganini requested that when she died her body should be cast into the deepest part of the D'Entrecasteaux Channel which runs between her home, Bruny Island, and the mainland. However, when Truganini died she was buried, and in 1878 her body was exhumed by the Royal Society of Tasmania and her skeleton was displayed in the society's museum. The sign beneath the skeleton said: 'Lallah Rooke or Truganini: The Last Tasmanian Aborigine.'

Her skeleton was also sent to Melbourne to be displayed. The skeleton was later removed from public display and kept in storage in the Hobart Museum. In 1977 it was cremated, and Truganini's ashes were scattered on the tribal fishing grounds of the South-east people.

Although Truganini has for many years been known as 'the last of the Tasmanian Aborigines', this title is now much disputed by some historians and by people who claim to be the descendants of the Tasmanian Aborigines.

VERONICA, St

The name 'Veronica' is composed of the words 'vera icon' and so has the meaning 'true image'. The story told of St Veronica is that she was a pious woman of Jerusalem who, filled with compassion at the sight of Christ as he laboured under the weight of the cross on his way to Calvary, wiped his face with a cloth. The image of Christ's face was left on the cloth, and the cloth is now preserved in St Peter's, Rome, where it has been since the eighth century. It would seem likely that Veronica is a fictitious, not an historical, character, probably invented to explain the existence of the relic known as 'The Veil of Veronica'. Feast day: 12 July.

XAVIER, ST FRANCIS (1506–51)

Francis was born in the castle of Xavier in Spanish Navarre, to a Basque family. He was educated in Paris where he became one of the seven men who, as the first Jesuits, took their vows at Montmartre in 1534, and were ordained priests in Venice three years later. Francis went as a missionary to Goa in Portuguese India in 1541. He also worked in Japan and in China where he became ill and died. His body was put in quicklime and taken to Goa where it remains enshrined and incorrupt. In 1615 his right arm was detached from his body and is in the church of the Gesu in Rome. His letters were long and detailed, and many of them have survived, giving a vivid impression of Francis and his life. He was canonized in 1622. Feast day: 3 December.

ligature *un*tapped

This print edition published in collaboration with Brio Books,
an imprint of Booktopia Group Ltd

Level 6, 1A Homebush Bay Drive · Rhodes NSW 2138 · Australia

Print ISBN: 9781761280801

briobooks.com.au

The paper in this book is FSC® certified.
FSC® promotes environmentally responsible,
socially beneficial and economically viable
management of the world's forests.

MIX
Paper from
responsible sources
FSC® C008194